QUICK

TENDER

BERT LINDSEY

Buried Stones Press
2019

ISBN 978-1-945506-07-9
1-945506-07-5

First Printing: 2018   Page Publishing
Printed in the United States of America

To the love of my life
Kathy Gale Bridges-Lindsey

CONTENTS

CHAPTER 1: THE ATTACK

Little did Quick Tender know that the time spent sewing torn sails on his grandfather's schooner would possibly save his life. He was losing more blood than he could afford. But first, he had to reload his two Colts.

The two things he had kept off the sinking schooner would indeed save his life: a sail sewing kit and a brass telescope.

Before being wounded, he had cautiously surveyed the spring-fed creek that would intersect Pecan Bayou, which would lead him to the low-river crossing on the Colorado. He had changed his plan to cross in the twilight and decided to wait on the moonlight, around ten o'clock to cross.

Quick had feared Indians might be watching the crossing in the late evening, and it would be safer to stay along the spring-fed creek and Pecan Bayou until after dark. It was only a short distance to the crossing. There, he would cross over to the west side. He could reach his destination in less than three hours, even at his planned, cautious speed.

After removing his saddle and bridle from his horse Echo, who rushed off to graze, he swung his saddlebags over his shoulder and stood erect with the saddle in hand. Echo let out a ferocious alert. Dropping his saddle and reaching for his guns, Quick was knocked forward by some unknown force in the direction of the creek bed. He turned in midair. Everything seemed in slow motion. He clearly saw five Indians rushing toward him.

The Colts belched fire, and two of them were dead before they hit the ground. Before Quick cleared the bank of the creek, a large arrow went completely through his upper thigh. He had felt no pain. Landing on his feet and crouching as planned, Quick took three steps to his left, stood erect, and fired three shots at the three approaching Indians. One bullet went between the eyes of each. Same as the previous two had received. Quick knew the target between the eyes was a mistake, but he could not afford for it to have been any other target.

Ducking again and silently moving several yards down the creek, Quick reloaded his Colts as he went. Before he stopped, he had thought of things that needed answers. Where were their horses? Was another Indian holding them? How far away was their main party? How many were in that party? Did they hear the shots?

He felt his leg becoming warm. Looking down and seeing all the blood brought the realization that he was wounded, and there was pain. He knew how important it was to move and move fast. But first things first, he had to stop the bleeding. Quick softly whistled for Echo. Out of nowhere, Echo appeared. Smelling blood and seeing the dead Indians, Echo was nervous before seeing Quick. Echo acknowledged Quick with a nod. Quick signaled Echo to go into a state of high alert. Echo moved out a short distance from the creek and took on his duties with eyes and ears darting in all directions.

Quick took one of his knives and ripped open his blood-soaked trousers. Seeing the two large gaping holes, he knew he had to work fast. Quick reached for his saddlebag that held the sail sewing kit and the brass telescope. Now he knew what had knocked him forward. A large arrow, aimed at his heart, hit the brass telescope. It stopped the arrow but pushed him forward toward the creek bed.

Quick removed the arrow and dug deep for the sewing kit. A large curved needle with enough thread was rapidly prepared. Quick cut off a willow branch, two feet long and one inch in diameter. Peeling it, then cutting it in half, Quick placed one in his mouth and bit down. He laid the other aside. Without cleaning or wiping away any blood, Quick buried the needle deep into his leg. Stopping, Quick took a deep breath and bit down harder. He then plunged the needle to the other side of the wound. He then started lacing.

When he had reached the bottom of the wound, he cross-stitched his way back to the beginning. Quick took his shirtsleeve and wiped the sweat from his face and eyes. Having destroyed the stick in his mouth, he removed it. Grabbing the other stick and thrusting it in his mouth, he started sewing on the exit wound of the arrow.

When finished, all the bleeding had stopped. Quick closed his eyes in total exhaustion. He knew not how much blood he had lost but knew if he had not had the needle and thread, he would have bled out.

Quick was not hungry, but to build up his blood supply, he forced himself to eat some of the jerky and several pieces of the raw bacon. He soon felt rewarding results.

After cutting strips from his shirttail, Quick placed the willow bark camber side down over the wounds and tied them with the strips. He slung his canteens and saddlebags over his shoulders and stood. Quick had to steady himself by grabbing hold of the willow tree. He waited until his head cleared and some of his strength had returned to his shaken body. In about fifteen minutes, Quick felt he had gained enough strength to climb out of the creek bed. The time recovering was also spent studying his surroundings and planning. After climbing out of the creek bed, Quick had to rest again before he could saddle Echo and remount.

He would not have the time or energy to hide or bury the Indians. He also knew the Comanche always removed their dead from the battleground. Them removing the dead would slow them down or possibly reduce their number in pursuit of him.

Quick softly called for Echo. He knew his leg was better now than it would be in a few hours when the swelling and stiffness set in. After saddling up, he began his search for the Indians' horses. About two hundred yards from the attack, he discovered five mustangs. He looked for any sign that others could have been present. Finding none, Quick wanted to release the mustangs. But for fear they would return to their camp and set off the search for the missing Indians, he decided to leave them tied.

The way Quick had it figured, the search for the dead Indians would not start until tomorrow. He had to find a defendable shelter and a place where he could hold up until his wounds healed. He knew he would have some infection, and no hard riding could be done for at least two or three weeks.

CHAPTER 2:
THE DETOUR

Earlier in the day that Quick was wounded, he had ridden through Goldthwaite pass. The pass led down to a new trading post he had heard of from a prospector back down the trail. Quick did not want to go through a town. His misfortune of having to kill four men, his escape from a jail, and having a bounty on his head, dead or alive, meant it was imperative for him to stay away from crowds and the law.

It had been his intention to restock his supplies and head north to DeLeon. White settlers had started moving into that area in 1854 after the Comanche had moved out of the area. Fort Shirley was near, at Flat Creek, to protect the settlement and wagon trains passing through to the west. The commander was Colonel Jack Freeman. The colonel was a friend and customer of his deceased grandfather, Captain Dag Drake. Captain Drake had picked up supplies for the colonel numerous times in New Orleans and carried them to Galveston. On several occasions, Colonel Freeman accompanied the supplies and was always a guest for dinner with Captain Drake and Quick. Colonel Freeman knew of Quick's mother and father's death. Quick wanted Colonel Freeman's advice on how to handle the situation he was in. After hearing his side of the story, it being a civil matter, he was sure the colonel would not turn him over to the local law.

Ray Stephens owned the trading post and traded with travelers heading west to the wide low-river crossing of the Colorado River. It lay about fifteen miles further west. He also traded with a few scattered settlers and the many friendly Indians. Quick studied the trading post before riding in, and it seemed deserted.

Stephens was startled to see Quick. For that matter, he would have been startled to see any white man traveling alone during the widespread Indian uprising that started two days before. The uprising was news to Quick. Seems the Comanche who left the area in the early 1850s had just returned. They were a nomadic tribe and had been on the warpath in northwest Texas.

Stephens had reports of several homesteaders being killed and burned out. Stephens was packing and moving out to De Leon to be near the fort, sixty miles north of Goldthwaite. He would stay until the raids ended, which could last several months, then move back if he had anything left to move back to.

Stephens had three Indians working for him: two Tonkawa and one Waco. Quick knew the Tonkawa language. The Tonkawa were friends and traders with the Cherokee and visited their camps often. Quick had a good conversation with the Tonkawa and signed with the Waco.

The Indians planned to leave Stephens in De Leon and go to their village north of Nacogdoches and wait out the uprising. The Waco had no safe route to his tribe and planned to join the Tonkawa.

Quick had a lot of faith in most Indians. They were always true to their word, especially the Cherokee and Tonkawa. Quick retrieved a letter from his saddlebag that was addressed to the Texas Rangers in Austin, Texas.

Quick pulled one of the Tonkawa aside and told him how important the letter was. He told him not to tell anyone about it and to mail it when he got to De Leon. The Tonkawa told Quick he appreciated the trust he placed in him, and that it would be done.

Stephens encouraged Quick to join him and his porters on their trip to De Leon. Quick politely declined. He did not want to go near De Leon or the fort, knowing there would be too many people and especially lawmen in the area. He would put off a meeting with Colonel Freeman. He also felt it would be safer for him to travel alone and fast.

Stephens expressed a desire to leave the area as soon as possible and asked for Quick's needs. Quick bought all the jerky that Stephens had left, which would last a week if that was all the food available. Jerky was great if you were in a hurry, which Quick would be. He also replenished his coffee and bacon. He was also able to buy a bundle of leather pig ties. Most people made their own from deer or the like, and he was surprised that Stephens had them for sale. He did not want to add any ammunition because of the weight. He did not waste ammunition and had enough to fight two or three Indian attacks for several days. Most of his surplus ammunition was wrapped in heavy cloth and covered with goose grease to repel any moisture.

Quick asked Stephens to draw him a map to the low river crossing. Stephens produced one already drawn in anticipation of the need for travelers going west. Stephens pointed out the spring creek. He warned Quick not to go into the swamp just west of the spring-fed creek, called Pecan Bayou, because of quicksand. He pointed out that the Indians would not dare go into the swamp either, and it would give Quick protection from any possible attack from the west.

Stephens had marked the crossing with an X on the map, which was just south of the large horseshoe curve on the Colorado.

Quick paid for his supplies, thanked Stephens for the map and information, then departed due west to intersect the small spring-fed creek. Quick had moved off the trail some fifty yards and continued looking back and to each side. He was traveling at a fast pace but stopped often to listen and look for signs.

CHAPTER 3: THE LOW-RIVER CROSSING

With the necessity of finding a defensible hideout, Quick decided to change back to his original plan and cross the Colorado as soon as possible. Quick cleaned his weapons and checked his wounds, then started west with the Henry lying across his saddle horn. Quick made no effort to cover his trail. He wanted distance.

He still felt sure he could make it to the Colorado in three hours. Echo moved swiftly and on high alert. Everything around them was still and quiet. Quick did not give in to the pain from his wound, which was telling him to stop and rest. To do so could result in his death. He pushed the urge to stop out of his mind and concentrated on the dangers that may be lurking ahead. The sun was beginning to go down, and shadows played tricks on Quick's eyes, forcing him to take second looks. Even Echo's ears darted up and around numerous times. Shortly, Echo came to a sudden stop with his head up and ears pointing ahead. Quick raised the Henry and grabbed the Colt from his belt. What Echo heard was the rumble of the water rushing over the low-river crossing of the Colorado.

Quick had to get across now before total darkness. He picked up the pace, hoping that any sounds he made would be confused with the rumbling water ahead. The trail led to the large horseshoe curve in the river and turned south toward the crossing. Quick remembered the horseshoe curve was where the Colorado changed direction. The river flowed from the west, and just past the large horseshoe curve, the flow changed to the south all the way to the Gulf of Mexico.

Echo showed no restraint in crossing, and Quick did not worry about his tracks entering the crossing. He wanted them seen going into the river and coming out because his plan was to cross back to the east side. Quick knew he had to continue until he reached his goal of a defendable hideout. After exiting the river, Quick found a place about two hundred yards away from the trail where he would wait for the moon to rise, giving him enough light to cross back across the river.

Quick had been so wrapped up in his escape that he had blocked out the pain from his wounds. Quick dismounted, removed Echo's saddle and bridle, and let him have a good roll. Putting Echo back on alert, Quick checked his weapons and turned his attention to his wounds.

The throbbing pain was with every heartbeat. He gently pulled down his pants. The leg was so swollen that he could not untie the bandages in the dark. Slipping out one of his knives, he glided the thin blade under the tied strip of cloth and cut it free, which gave instant relief. The pain was still present, but the throbbing had ceased. Lifting the watertight tin from his shirt pocket, he removed a match and lit it behind a shielded hand. He removed the bark. Seeping fluids were present. The stitches had tightened due to the swelling, and this alone was causing much of the pain. The cool breeze gave some relief. Other than the swelling, it looked better than he'd imagined it would. He loosely retied the bark. As soon as the moon comes out, he had to find his hideout.

Even though he was not hungry, Quick ate two strips of jerky and drank more water than he wanted. He then checked his weapons and placed them where he could find them in the dark.

With the security of knowing Echo would alert him to any danger, he closed his eyes and went to sleep. As he awoke from a couple of hours of restless sleep, Quick lay still. He listened and let his eyes adjust to the darkness.

Convinced he was alone, Quick retrieved and checked his weapons. He then softly whistled for Echo. Within minutes, Quick had Echo saddled and moving out of the brush back to the trail. The trail was wide and had numerous tracks of horses, wagons, and livestock. Some had deep impressions created by pack animals. The moon was just coming out, and the deeper impressions were easier seen by the shadows they created.

Quick headed west on the trail for a quarter of a mile and worked over to the south side edge of the trail. Diverting from the trail, he led Echo at an angle and turned him around, carefully covering all tracks that were off the trail. Before heading back to the low-water crossing, Quick gathered a small bundle of dead mesquite branches and tied them on the back of the saddle with a lariat.

When Quick arrived at the low-river crossing, he turned Echo north at the edge of the river and headed toward the horseshoe bend. Quick was continuously looking back, making sure the swift water was filling Echo's tracks with gravel and sand. When the river began turning in the horseshoe, Quick had a clear view of the north shore. Quick saw a place to his liking to cross back to the northeast side. He knew the swift water would sweep Echo down the river at least five hundred yards before reaching the desired exit point. Quick moved on around the curve, making sure Echo could reach the exit point in time.

The moon was now shining bright. Quick turned Echo to the northeast, and Echo stopped to look back at him. With a flick of the reins, Echo obeyed and moved forward into the swift water.

About ten yards out, Echo stepped off a ledge and was swept away by the current. Water went up to Quick's waist. He instantly raised the Henry over his head, keeping the rifle dry.

To make it easier on Echo, Quick slipped from the saddle, hanging on with his left hand, and continued holding the Henry out of the water with his right. He would guide Echo by lightly tapping on the right side of Echo's neck with the butt of the Henry.

Things went well until Echo hit bottom on the east side. Quick had to remount now! He had much pain and difficulty getting his wounded leg back over the saddle. The bundle of brush did not help. Regardless of the pain, he had to remount.

Quick could feel the tearing of flesh as he forced the remount, but remount he did. When Quick reached the bank, a ring of fresh blood was visible and getting larger. He had anticipated the need to cover Echo's tracks leaving the river and untied the bundle of mesquite and dropped it behind Echo as he was leaving the river's edge. The bundle pulled sand and gravel into Echo's tracks as if he had never been there. Away from the river, the bundle of mesquite was added to the driftwood along the shore.

There was a large cliff overlooking the river at the top of the horseshoe bend. About halfway up the skirt of the cliff, Quick saw a small plateau that he had not seen from down below. He rode closer into the cliff until a previous rockslide blocked the way. He rode further up the cliff but saw no trail; he turned around to go back. Then he saw it. A five-foot section of an old trail was all he saw. It was grown over and seemed to have not been used in years.

He would have liked to explore it on foot but was too weak. He eased Echo to the trail, and in a short distance, they were on the plateau. It was bigger than it looked when he first saw it. There was a water seep in the west corner. Berries were growing as well as much greener vegetation. The plateau was blocked off from the west, and there was a large protruding rock structure overhanging the plateau.

Quick led Echo to the edge of the plateau where he could see the river fifty yards below in both directions. The only entrance was the one he came in on. There was no cave, just a few indentions that sunk back into the face of the cliff.

He chose the one closest to the entrance of the plateau. He would make this his camp. The location could not be seen from above, below, or from the west. It could only be seen from the trail leading in, and he would always lie or sit facing that direction. It was also protected from the east by the quicksand in the Pecan Bayou. Quick was pleased.

Quick dismounted and poured water from his canteen into his hat to offer it to Echo. He was not interested. Quick then began removing his gear and the saddle. Echo went straight to the seep, began digging with his hooves, and was drinking within minutes.

Quick unloaded his weapons and cleaned them. He placed all the wet ammunition in an old sock and got out some of his ammunition that was packed in the watertight goose-grease-covered packages. He reloaded all his pistols and cleaned his knives.

Quick's thoughts went back to the killings. He felt some remorse about the Indians, even though the Comanche were a vicious tribe and had intended to kill him. He felt no remorse for the four white men. All the killings were a life-or-death situation for him, and he had been taught to move on and no longer dwell on them.

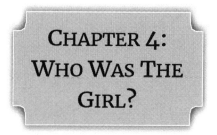

CHAPTER 4:
WHO WAS THE GIRL?

His leg needed attention and time to heal. Quick estimated he had at least four hours before daylight. He set out to remove his wet boots. After removing the right boot, he knew he had to cut off the left. The swelling from his wound had now encompassed his entire leg. He reached for his thin knife, made a slit down both sides of the boot, and lifted his foot free. After drying his feet, he slipped on his moccasins.

Quick took off the bark and could see the wound in the moonlight. It had stopped bleeding but was extremely swollen. Two of the stitches had torn through the flesh when he had to remount. The wound was open in that area with no flesh intact to tie on to. Quick pulled the wet torn trousers away from his leg, dried the wound best as he could, and laid the bark gently back over the wound, and tied it down loosely. Quick placed his weapons and closed his eyes.

The next morning, using the Henry as a crutch, he searched for the perfect limb to make a sturdier crutch. After finding one that would work, he went back to the hideout and whittled it out to perfection.

Using the crutch, Quick went to the seep. He had worried that the seep might dry up. Using his bowie knife and hands, he cut out a trench one yard long, two feet wide, and one foot deep to create a small reservoir. The trench was full in less than ten minutes. After filling up his canteens at the seep, Quick returned to his camp with an armful of dry wood. He decided to cook all the bacon and boil a full pot of coffee, being that this would be the last fire he could safely build. After cooking the bacon and boiling the coffee, Quick boiled one of his wet shirts to sanitize it and use it for bandages. Quick built the fire under a thick mesquite tree to disperse any smoke. When the bacon and coffee were ready, Quick ate and drank as much as he could. He then separated the burning limbs and buried them deep, eliminating any chance of smoke or odor escaping.

With the aid of his crutch, Quick went back down the trail and wiped out all tracks of his entry, then returned to his camp.

Quick checked all his weapons and then eased up to the edge of the plateau. It was still early in the morning, and he did not expect any Indians until later in the evening or early the next day. After looking over the edge of the plateau from several locations, Quick selected the one that would give him the best advantage. Knowing the only entry to the cliff was the trail he had followed in, he chose a location where he could see up, down, and across the river, and cover the trail. Quick was careful not to move anything on the face of the cliff. He found a place between two large stones that gave him a good view. This would be his lookout. Quick settled in and studied the terrain for two hours. He considered every tree, rock, clump of grass, and shadow. He would do the same at noon, evening, and the next morning. He estimated distances of natural structures and wind directions.

Quick left a full canteen and returned to his camp area. If the Indians came, he wanted it before any infection kicked in. He could handle the pain but had no control over the effects of fever.

Echo was content with his surroundings; he had plenty of water and needed the rest. Quick had restricted Echo to the rear of the plateau with signals. Echo had no need to go to the front of the cliff anyway.

After eating more bacon and drinking a cup of cold coffee, Quick placed his weapons and closed his eyes. It was hard to go to sleep when in pain, but not so much when you're exhausted. Quick went to sleep. Around noon, he awoke.

Easing out to his lookout, he followed the previous procedure and paid attention to the noon shadows. He repeated the procedure later in the evening, then returned to camp.

Quick began to feel hot. He removed the bark to see the inflamed, bloody mess. He needed to clean the wound but did not trust building a fire. The coffee in the pot had been boiled. He did not know if it was the right thing to do but felt that he had no alternative. He cut off a section of the boiled shirt and saturated it with the coffee. He then gently rubbed it around the edges of the wound. He then took the bark and washed it off with the water from the canteen, then rinsed it with the cold coffee and placed it back over the wound. He then closed his eyes.

Quick woke up several hours later, startled. He was freezing, and his teeth were chattering so loudly that he had been woken by Echo, who was now standing over him. Quick dug out his coat and blanket and wrapped it around himself. Then he stood for several hours with his arms wrapped around Echo to steal some of his body heat. His clothes were wet from the sweat created by the fever. Quick spent the rest of the night suffering from chills and fever.

Not knowing where the Indians had their camp, there was no way to be certain where they would find Quick's trail. It was likely they found it before dark yesterday and would be hot on it this morning.

Quick eased to his lookout site. As daylight approached, Quick started scanning the landscape. He was soon able to determine that nothing had changed in the appearance of the rocks, trees, or shadows. Quick was a very patient person. He had experienced not moving for hours at a time. However, that was without wounds, pain, and fever. The pain in his leg was now taking most of his attention, and he was burning up with fever. After easing down from his lookout, he moved back to his camp. Quick took a needed drink, then wet his bandana and placed it over his closed eyes.

He had been gone from the lookout for at least an hour when he noticed the fever had seemed to subside.

Then, all hell seemed to have broken loose down below. Echo came running toward Quick and stopped in his tracks upon seeing Quick's signal to stop. The shooting and yelling were continuing as Quick checked his weapons and moved to his lookout. Across the river and to his right, he saw two horses, a man and a girl. They had their backs to the river and were behind a log, firing at shadows and Indians.

Quick located eleven Indians closing in around the couple and immediately formed a plan. The Henry was very accurate from two hundred yards. He had shot the Henry for hours from the crow's nest, with the schooner underway and rolling in the waves. Hitting targets, in rapid concession, until the fifteen-shot Henry was empty was always expected by the crew.

He would start shooting the Indians at the rear of the attack, not letting the ones in front know that their party was being wiped out. He felt he had no choice but to use the same target. All the shots from the Indians and the couple would camouflage his shots.

Quick took a deep breath and started firing. Everything went as planned. It took less than twenty seconds and eleven shots. All eleven Indians were dead from a single shot between the eyes.

Quick began breathing again and reloaded his Henry. He was sure there had been only eleven Indians below but looked again to make sure.

The man and woman were looking for more Indians. They seemed confused as to what had just happened. They must have thought they had killed all the Indians. They had never looked back up the cliff from which Quick had been firing.

The couple was about seventy yards away, fifty yards across the river, and twenty yards up the river from him. With the help of the crutch, Quick stood up, whistled, and waved. The man and woman were startled and hesitant. Quick signaled them to come closer so they could talk.

Grabbing their horses, they rode up until they were across the river from him. It was evident to Quick that the man was much older than the girl. The girl!

His first thought was that he had to look terrible, with a full beard, ragged clothes, and leaning on a crutch in pain. So much for first impressions! That was now over, and she was so beautiful.

How could he be thinking anything about a girl while being in so much pain? He was burning up with fever. He could be killed any time for the bounty or killed by the Indians. But she was all he could think about. What could such a beautiful girl be doing with such a sleazy-looking man?

Quick asked if they were okay and was answered with a yes. As bad as he hated to ask for help, he did. He told them he was wounded and needed help. He told them of his secure hide-out and provisions, and that he would greatly reward them for their help. "Will you please help me?"

The girl replied, "Yes," without hesitation. The man held up his hand and halted the conversation with, "We will discuss it in private." He turned his horse and motioned to the girl to follow. As

26

the girl turned to follow, she looked back over her shoulder and held a long stare with Quick. They rode up the river and dismounted. Quick saw them argue. The only thing he could make out was San Angelo.

The young girl got on her horse and turned back toward Quick. Before she could leave, the man jerked her off the horse and slapped her to the ground. He then put her back on her horse. After a frightened look back at Quick, she was led away. The man had a tight hold on the reins. As she was led away, Quick lowered the Henry that had been sighted between the man's eyes.

All the girl's thoughts were on this man. Who was he? Why was she thinking of him rather than how she was just struck to the ground? Was it because she felt sorry for him? Why would that make her knees weak? He didn't act as though he wanted them to feel sorry for him. It could have been that even wounded and leaning on a crutch, he looked in total command. Why did this thought make her heart beat faster? Maybe it was the thought that he might be able to help her with her uncle.

Quick's heart ached as he made his way back to his camp. His fever was beginning to rise. Echo seemed to know Quick was in bad shape and nervously stood by. Sitting down, he reached out and rubbed Echo's nose to keep him calm. Quick then signaled Echo to stay close and quiet.

Quick wet his bandana and placed it over his burning eyes as he drifted to sleep. It was dark when he awoke with chills. He was frightened by the sound of his teeth chattering uncontrollably. He knew it could be heard from quite a distance. He immediately drew his bowie knife and cut a limb from the mesquite. He trimmed up a section and bit down, silencing the chatter.

He knew not what time it was, but being a student of the sky, he estimated it was close to daylight. If so, he had been out for about eighteen hours. He felt better even though his teeth were digging into the mesquite with their repetitive silent action. He knew this was not over.

After checking all his weapons, he drank his fill from the canteen. He forced himself to eat some bacon and drink more of the cold coffee. He trimmed several limbs from the mesquite and replaced the original.

Quick's thoughts went to the only pleasant thing he had experienced in quite some time: the girl. He had known lots of girls, from southern belles in New Orleans that wanted the world to spin around them to Indian maidens who would do anything to please their man.

Why was he so impressed with this girl? He knew nothing about her, nor had he even talked with her. He had never given any other girl a second thought. All he knew was that she could shoot, ride a horse, and she wanted to help him.

What was she doing with that man? He feared for her safety from him. He wished now he had killed him. Quick was shocked at himself for thinking such a thing. Why did he have that thought? He knew immediately. The man had hit the only girl he had ever loved, and he did nothing to protect her. He felt foolish for thinking such, but he knew it was true.

He had never been in love. How did he know of such a thing? How could such a thing happen to him when all his attention should be on his survival? Now everything was focused on her survival.

He had to have a new plan. He wanted to be at his lookout before daylight to check his surroundings. He crawled out with plenty of time to spare. As it got lighter, he saw, to no surprise, there were no dead Indians in sight. No movement or sound. Just disturbed earth around the bloodstained ground where the dead had been loaded and hauled away. It must have happened the evening before.

A crushing realization came to mind. The Comanche would surely be after the girl and her companion. Quick's heart raced. He wanted to leave at that moment but knew it was impossible. He never once thought the Indians had killed or captured the girl. He had blind faith that it was a fact. He also knew he would find her as soon as he could ride.

Crawling back to his camp, he checked the wound. To his surprise, it looked much better. He had been careful to keep the leg straight. He decided to keep the willow bark and bandages off in the day and let the wound dry out. He would cover it loosely at night.

He wanted to know everything about the girl. He was concerned about what to tell the girl about himself, as well. He did not want the past to interfere with the future, but he had to tell her the truth.

He wanted to remember everything about his past and lay it out in the open. The best place to start was at the beginning, as told to him by his grandfather and his memory. Now the truth.

CHAPTER 5:
THE BEGINNING

Quick was born in Cut and Shoot, Texas, which is approximately one hundred and forty miles north of Galveston. His parents were Pete and Abby Gale Tender. Pete and Abby Gale owned a sawmill that cut mining timbers. They shipped them to Mexico by boat and freight wagons.

Pete and Abby Gale were having their first child. Abby Gale's father, Captain Dag Drake, and mother, Mary Sue, came from Galveston with Nez, their Cherokee Indian housekeeper, to be present for the birth. Nez decided to leave her younger daughter with a family member.

Complications during the birth resulted in Abby Gale's death. The baby survived. Mary Sue and Nez set out to find a nursing surrogate mother. Success was found in a large Cherokee village east of Cut and Shoot.

Pete was not much of a drinker, but the pain was more than he could handle. Cut and Shoot had two saloons, the Flying Rooster and the Misty Hollow. Pete had gone to the Misty Hollow and downed two shots of rye, then ordered a third. Two of the Cut and Shoot toughies, the Cole brothers, Melvin and Christy, came in. They knew Pete and did not seem to care for him.

Pete did not hang out in the saloons, and the brothers were surprised to see him there. They insisted Pete sit with them, buy them a drink, and tell them why he did not like them. Pete refused and went to the Flying Rooster. The Cole brothers followed and cornered him. They accused him of thinking he was too good to drink with them and made threats to kill him.

Pete tried to talk his way out of his bad situation, even to the point of trying to give them his gun. As he reached to give the gun to them, the brothers shot Pete numerous times, killing him. The sheriff was Melvin and Christy's first cousin, Brandon Cole. Sheriff Cole determined the killing was self-defense. He had done this twice before for killings that Melvin and Christy had committed.

Mary Sue and Nez stayed in the village that night. Early the next morning, an Indian who worked at the sawmill came with the news that Pete had been killed. Mary Sue left Nez in the village with the baby and returned to Cut and Shoot to assist Captain Drake. They buried their daughter and Pete and sold their house and sawmill.

Captain Drake returned to Galveston, and Mary Sue returned to the Indian village to be with Nez and her grandson. When the baby could make it without the aid of the surrogate, Captain Drake came for them, and they all returned to Galveston.

When the baby settled in, he would crawl around the house so quickly that Nez and Mary Sue had a hard time catching him. He had not been given a name, so "Quick" it was.

After a short while, it was determined that Quick was ambidextrous. He could handle any task equally well with either hand.

Nez and her young daughter were constant companions of Quick for the first four years of his life. He learned the Cherokee language before English. Nez always took Quick and her daughter to her family tribe for long visits. Quick was welcome to enter their games, hunts, and tracking outings.

The Cherokee were peace-loving farmers, nut gatherers, fishermen, trappers, and hunters. Quick enjoyed every minute spent with the Cherokee and developed a deep love and affection for the Cherokee people and their culture. The Cherokee always looked forward to Quick's visits. They treated him as one of their own.

Quick was six-years-old when his grandmother died of consumption. Captain Drake moved Quick on board his schooner and made a plan that would give him an education far superior to any in existence.

The schooner hauled passengers and freight, which included carriages and horses. The vessel made stops in New Orleans, Sabine Pass, Galveston, Port Lavaca, and Corpus Christi. The ship had three masts and a small wood-fired steam engine used in and around ports.

Captain Drake was a tough and stern man. He treated people square and expected the same. He required all gamblers and floozy women to report to him upon boarding the schooner. They were told that any gambler caught cheating would be thrown overboard, no second chances. Any floozy woman caught carousing or applying her trade would be locked up and put off in the next port.

Quick was present for many of these meetings and witnessed the consequence. Never did Captain Drake listen to any argument. Quick was exposed to people from all over the world, from all backgrounds and cultures.

Each night, Captain Drake and Quick would have dinner in his cabin, often with guests. Captain Drake, being from Sweden, spoke many languages. Not only Swedish and the Swedes' five sub-languages, but also English, German, French, Portuguese, Spanish, Chinese, and Russian. Quick did not participate in conversations unless he was asked a question. Quick hung on to every spoken word, mannerism, and accent. After guests left, Captain Drake answered all of Quick's questions. Captain Drake would point out on maps, which were always handy, the different countries, territories, or areas mentioned in the dinner conversations.

Captain Drake had liked Quick's father. He had always known him as an honest businessman and a good husband that took good care of his daughter. He stressed these things with Quick, while also pointing out on numerous occasions that because his father was not prepared to defend himself, he was murdered.

Captain Drake was determined that Quick would be prepared to defend himself. Captain Drake instructed Quick to mind his own business. He pointed out there were times and things that could happen that would make it his business. Quick should always let people know that he was not looking for trouble but was prepared to defend himself. To do so, he had to learn how.

Captain Drake considered every hand on deck as a defender of life, cargo, and ship. Pirates still applied their trade in the Gulf of Mexico. Captain Drake's schooner and crew had a reputation of defeating every attack that was ever attempted and leaving the attackers in ruins. When pirates recognized the schooner, they turned away to seek easier prey.

CHAPTER 6:
SELF DEFENSE

Captain Drake made the plan for Quick's training. He assigned Jo Ling to carry out the plan. Jo Ling was a small-framed man in his thirties. He was the Segundo of the schooner. He was well-liked by all the crew and respected for his knowledge of worldly affairs and his mastery of speaking the English language without an accent. Only the crew knew of his skills in body control, leverage, bone and joint structure, and above all, his ability to kill with his bare hands.

Day and night, for months, Jo Ling taught Quick the Asian art of death, injury, and escapes, using no more than his knowledge and body. Quick became a steward of this knowledge to be used for protection and death if required.

Jo Ling stressed to Quick the importance of keeping secret all his training. He should never be known as a man that had all the skills that he had or would be acquiring. He told Quick that with the way the world was heading, he would more than likely be forced to use these skills and likely take a life. This should be avoided if possible, but never hesitate if in a life-or-death situation. He was to tell himself it was a life-or-death situation and move on.

Under Jo Ling's guidance, Rafiel Fazio, who was called Fazio by the crew, taught acrobatics. Quick had seen Fazio swinging from mast to mast and effortlessly climb in and out of the ropes that supported the sails. He saw Fazio swing from the crow's nest, let go in midair, grab ropes on the way down, turn a flip, and land at Quick's feet. Quick was given a regimen of exercises and feats to be accomplished daily, under Fazio's supervision.

Boris Crewcheck was appointed to teach Quick about knives, their many uses, care, and handling. Boris, as he was called by the crew, always had a knife up every sleeve, in both boots, on his hips, behind his neck, and behind his belt in the back. He had them to dig, throw, cut, saw, pick, and to kill. They were well balanced, held the finest edge, and were made of the finest carbon steel.

Quick learned the dos and don'ts of knife fighting. At the end of three months of training, Boris presented Quick with a knife for his holster, boot, neck, and one for each sleeve. Quick and the knives were inseparable. Boris and Jo Ling practiced daily with Quick on the arts and skills he was being taught.

Captain Drake knew the dregs of the world could be found around every port in the world. Many had been run out of their country by the law or escaped the law by way of the sea. Defense of the body was of the utmost importance. All education would contribute greatly in planning and expectations of self-defense. He was not paranoid, but he had taught himself to always expect the unexpected. Quick was now seven years old. It was time to expand his reading and self-defense training.

By age eight, Quick was reading everything on the ship. Quick sought out conversations that passengers were having in Spanish and French. He would listen in an inconspicuous manner. He marveled at the flow of words and gestures of the participants.

By age nine, Quick was climbing to the crow's nest using only his hands. He would then rappel down using the mast structures. He wrestled with Jo Ling daily and even managed to escape from him occasionally. He continued his knife practices and his evening history, geography, and map studies. He was now carrying on conversations in Spanish and French with Captain Drake.

Jo Ling appointed Ross Boudreaux, who was called Ross by the crew, to teach Quick about locks, pickpockets, and cards. Ross's job on the schooner was to watch over the gambling and eliminate the cheaters before trouble started and to pick the pockets of all the pickpockets and eliminate them.

Quick learned how cheats marked cards, dealt from the bottom, dealt seconds or thirds, stacked the deck, skipped the cut, dropped a hand, and made signals to a shill. Ross gave Quick his first deck of cards and taught him odds and money management. After six months of practice for at least six hours each day, Quick mastered the game. He was now a card mechanic with either hand.

Ross also taught Quick the art of picking pockets and illusions. He pointed out that he might need this art at any time. Being ambidextrous, he took to it like a duck takes to water. This was an enjoyable art that Quick practiced on the crew for fun.

Ross had many words of wisdom. One was that cheats always had a hidden gun. If they got caught, they would try to use it. He told Quick to never confront the cheat. The cheat would be so busy covering up his cheating he would not be watching him, and the cheat could then be turned into the mark.

Captain Drake dined with Quick nightly, discussing his progress. With this being Quick's tenth birthday, Jo Ling was asked by Captain Drake to join them on this evening. Captain Drake expressed his satisfaction with Quick's progress and Jo Ling's tutorage. He also expressed a sense of urgency that the training to be sped up, but not to the point that anything would be left out. Captain Drake suggested the solution would be personal hands-on training and an increase in hours. Quick was eager to increase his training and to increase the time spent to get it all completed. Jo Ling said he would arrange for

Paul Graham to work with Quick day and night to transfer his vast knowledge of guns, explosives, and the psychology of using both.

Paul's regular duties would be shared by the rest of the crew, but he would always be near if needed. Paul knew Quick was a great student and a fast learner. There was a lot to learn, and the practice would take a tremendous amount of time. Paul wasted no time diving in.

First thing was to have all firearms fully loaded. Paul pointed out that most people left the barrel of their guns empty for fear of shooting themselves. This left them at a single disadvantage and could get them killed for the lack of one bullet. Immediately after shooting, replace the spent shells. This was to be done even in battle. If one fired one shot, and if there is time, replace the one shot. Don't wait! It could mean one's life.

Paul explained that these questions were the same if in a city or a desert, a small room, or a large barn. Knowing the answers to these questions before trouble starts will give time to come up with a plan. Paul pointed out that guns were for killing. He emphasized the importance of determining not only who had the fastest shot but also who the leader was. The fastest should be killed first, but keep in mind that if the leader was killed, others might flee, especially if they feared getting paid. Hesitating on making this decision would get one killed.

Paul's favorite target was the head, between the eyes. This was always instant death, with no retaliation. One could move to the next target without fear of being shot by the first.

Quick learned all makes, calibers, shell capacity, and shooting distances of all pistols, rifles, shotguns, and artillery.

Paul discussed cannons, dynamite, gunpowder, and nitroglycerin at length. He also explained how to build explosive weapons and ways of triggering such.

When on land, Paul gave Quick extensive training in tracking and covering tracks. Paul was impressed with Quick's previous knowledge of the subject that he had picked up from his many visits to his Indian family.

When Quick was eleven and one-half years old, five foot six inches tall, and was one hundred sixty pounds of long, lean muscle, Paul gave him his first guns: two Colt .45-caliber pistols. Quick looked comfortable and much older than he was while wearing the Colts. Quick had filed off the front site of one of the Colts so it would not hang on his belt when he was drawing the pistol. He then shoved the pistol behind his belt in front, to be drawn with his left hand, with the other hanging on his right hip. His large bowie knife was on his left hip.

Paul spent countless hours with Quick, handling both guns. At twelve, they were loaded. Soon, Quick felt naked unless he had both guns in place. When it was time to fire his first shot, he was very comfortable. Even small targets seemed large and stood out in all situations, including shadows and bright sun.

When Quick reached thirteen years old, his bullets fired rapidly and landed where intended, even at moving targets. When he and the target were moving, it made no difference; it was a direct hit.

Paul then introduced the .44-caliber Henry rifle. It carried fifteen bullets and was extremely accurate at two hundred yards. The pistol training carried over to the Henry, and Quick could shoot it like a pistol at short distances. Brought to the shoulder, with the advantage of accuracy and the shots available without reloading, it was the very best weapon available for distance.

Captain Drake had been shipping the limited supply of Henry firearms and ammunition for the government. He had bartered for a case of the Henrys as well as an ample supply of .44 ammunition. He knew of no individual that had possessed the Henry, only the government.

Paul stressed to always have a plan. In battle, try to always do the unexpected. If on the ground, roll to the left because most people would roll to the right. Make doing the unexpected part of the plan. Part of one's plans was to always observe potential danger and react accordingly. Do this every day, all day. It's part of the plan. In battle, one will be shot at. Do not let it interfere with the overall plan.

CHAPTER 7:
THE GROWING YEARS

Quick observed that the country was getting rougher by the day. It was not unusual to see fistfights, knife fights, and shootings numerous times a week. Most of them occurred because one in the fight showed weakness. Wolves and coyotes look for the weak to attack, same with people. It was exactly what happened to his father.

Quick grew more determined to never let it happen to him. "Never show weakness" was burned into his brain. To balance this frame of mind was the constant reminder of Captain Drake. Always mind one's own business, try to avoid trouble, and never be known as a gunman.

Every day brought confidence, and with confidence, brought happiness. He was well built, handsome, and always had a slight smile on his face. This confused most people. What did this ever-present smile mean? Was he happy all the time? Not likely. Does he know something I don't know? Maybe. Is it about me? Could be. Without saying a word, those questions brought about the desire of men and women to want to know him. Their interest in wanting to know the answer often attracted them to him like a magnet to steel. Quick was selective in making himself available to divulge anything about himself. If he did, it was only inconsequential information. Knowledge was something that no one could take from him. He entertained himself by watching people. It could be a fistfight, an argument, or a lovers' quarrel. It was fun watching their actions and predicting the outcome.

While on the schooner, his favorite place was in the crow's nest. He would go there two or three times a day just for the fun of it. Each time, he would race to the top using only his hands and descend at a very rapid pace. His long, lean muscles had developed like ropes of steel. He glided throughout the mast with the movement of butter on a hot biscuit.

Quick was now fifteen years old. He stood five feet eleven and weighed one hundred and ninety pounds. Captain Drake continued to council Quick on many matters, but now was the time to include money and women.

Quick was taught to keep money in the form of gold, which would always have value. Captain Drake pointed out that paper money could be worth no more than the paper it was printed on. His favorite depository was Wells Fargo; you could have instant access throughout the country. He also pointed out that you should keep on hand enough gold to take advantage of any lucrative business deal that might require money in hand.

Quick was eager to know more about women. He had found that they were difficult to figure out. He did know that they could start more trouble than most men could handle, and some situations could lead to fistfights or even killings.

Captain Drake kept it simple. "Women want things that were hard to get, especially men. And they want to be protected by men. That's it in a nutshell. There is much more, but it is too difficult to explain and would confuse you because it is not constant. So be protective of the woman you want and be hard to get, and then everything else will fall into place." Captain Drake's advice bid him well.

Many hours were spent on geography. Special attention was given to Texas, the Indian Territory, New Mexico, Colorado, Arizona, Nevada, and California. Captain Drake would test Quick every night on geography. Quick could visualize all the southwest, even with never having laid eyes on it.

Quick had returned numerous times with Nez and her daughter to her village throughout the years. It was on one of those trips that he found Echo. He belonged to Big Lobo, whom he had known from childhood. Quick wanted to buy Echo. Lobo offered to trade Echo for the Henry rifle. This was one thing Quick would not do.

Quick had wrestled Lobo in his younger years. Lobo was three years older and had thirty pounds more weight than Quick. At that time, Quick never wanted to hurt or embarrass Lobo and always let him win. Quick struck a deal with Lobo. He would wrestle Lobo, and if he lost, he would give him the Henry and one of his Colts. If he won, he would get Echo. Lobo eagerly accepted. Quick felt guilty about this deal, but he really wanted this horse. He had known Echo since his birth. He had played with Echo throughout the years. Echo would come running anytime Quick entered the village.

He knew Lobo was the wrestling champion of not only his village but of the three neighboring villages. Everyone wanted to see this match, even though they felt sure that Lobo would win. Lobo had never been beaten, and Quick did not want to be known as the man that had beaten him. He would have to wrestle every Indian in the country who wanted to beat the man that had beaten Big Lobo.

He had to make this look as if he lucked out. Quick let Lobo have the advantage and would barely escape. This went on for over an hour. Quick had barely escaped from match-ending pins numerous times, often to the last second. It happened as planned. Quick got lucky and pinned Lobo.

The village had a great time, except Lobo. Quick admitted he got lucky, and a rematch was offered on his next visit. To ease his guilt, Quick gave Big Lobo five twenty-dollar gold pieces. Quick then left with Echo.

CHAPTER 8: HARD REALIZATIONS

Quick had just turned seventeen, reaching six-foot one-inch tall and weighing two-hundred and twenty pounds. He was bursting his seams with confidence when Captain Drake disclosed to Quick a secret he had hidden because he did not want to show a sign of weakness; out of necessity, now had to be the time.

Captain Drake disclosed to Quick that he too was dying of consumption, the wasting disease that had killed his grandmother. He now only had a short time to live.

Quick was shocked. He owed his grandfather so much and loved him and his guidance. He immediately realized that he would have no family left. He would have a house, but no home. He would have Jo Ling and the crew and Nez and her tribe, but it was not the same, regardless of how much he cared for them. He had no one!

Quick tried to express these feelings to Captain Drake and was interrupted.

"Quick, never show weakness," said Captain Drake. "Everyone will die sometime. You have been guided to this time in your life. You have the things you need to survive and to have an abundant life, including your future family."

It was time to share with Quick where all the family assets were. To Quick's amazement, his mother and father's home and sawmill sold for thirty thousand dollars. The money was converted into gold and deposited with Wells Fargo in Quick's name. Since Quick was Captain Drake's only heir, he had also deposited one million dollars of gold into his Wells Fargo account. Captain Drake had recently transferred railroad stock certificates from two railroad companies into Quick's name as well. Years back, he realized that the railroads were the future of the country. He bought thousands of cheap shares before the roads were built and many more before proven to be the success they turned out to be. He bought additional shares with dividends he received, once profits were made by the companies.

Captain Drake gave Quick all the paperwork to access his Wells Fargo account. He had added Quick's name to all his checking accounts. The money was not crucial to Quick now but was sure it would be in the future.

Some six months later, Captain Drake became ill while in port at Galveston. He became more ill when a government defense attaché came aboard and told Captain Drake that they were confiscating his schooner for national defense. The reason given for the confiscation was that the Confederate Army had used it to their advantage in the war. Captain Drake had never, to his knowledge, done business with the Confederacy and knew this was a carpetbagger ploy to get the schooner.

Captain Drake, with Quick and the crew present, ordered the attaché off the schooner and not to come back. The attaché assured Captain Drake that he would be back with force enough to take it. He was immediately escorted off the schooner.

Captain Drake told the crew that he was not going to let a bunch of carpetbaggers take the schooner and that he had a plan that would not involve them. He told them of his illness and his short time to live, and that he did not want to ruin their lives on a lost cause. The crew wanted to stay and fight. He instead gave them an order to prepare the schooner for setting sail and for them to depart the schooner.

As each departed, Captain Drake gave each three thousand dollars in gold coins. Each saluted Captain Drake and shook Quick's hand. Quick made sure that each had his address in Galveston and asked that each let him know how to reach them. He assured them he would get in touch with them as soon as he carried out Captain Drake's plan and things settled down afterward. Quick expressed that they were the only family he would have and never wanted to lose touch with them. They assured Quick that if needed, they would always be at his service.

After the crew left the schooner, Captain Drake had Quick fire up the steam engine and then take the schooner out into the bay. He then had him set sail into the gulf where there was no traffic. Anchor was set.

Captain Drake discussed with Quick how he wanted to be buried at sea, and that under no circumstances did he want the schooner to fall into the hands of the Yankee carpetbaggers. This feeling had been created when the attaché announced that the schooner would be confiscated without a hearing, discussion, or trial.

Captain Drake knew they would be on their way to attempt the confiscation. He went over the things that needed to be done before they arrived. Quick assured his grandfather that the schooner would not fall into their hands. Quick went below and strategically placed three kegs of gunpowder below the waterline and ran a long fuse above deck. The schooner's lifeboat was lowered to the water and tied off.

Quick then spent time comforting his grandfather above deck. In the distance, Quick spotted a flotilla consisting of five boats heading his way. Using Captain Drake's telescope, he saw that each carried ten men. Half of them carried shotguns as well as pistols and rifles. This show of force was to intimidate and force surrender without firing a shot. Little did they know, thought Quick.

Quick picked up his grandfather and slid down the rope with him in his arms. He comfortably lay him in the boat. Quick then climbed back up the rope to the deck. He had plenty of time to complete the tasks laid out by Captain Drake. He emptied the safe into a canvas bag, along with the sail sewing kit. Back on the deck, he saw the flotilla, with sails full, speeding ahead.

Quick grabbed the rope and slid back into the boat. He checked on his grandfather, making sure he was comfortable, then stored the bag and sewing kit. He wanted to make sure he had his timing right. He took one last look through the telescope. He cut off three feet of fuse, lit the remainder, and shoved off.

Immediately raising the sail and catching the same wind the flotilla had, Quick sped away about three hundred yards from the schooner. Quick's small boat had far greater speed than the flotilla. He turned the boat facing the schooner so he and Captain Drake would have a full view. He then lowered the sail. When the flotilla was within two hundred yards of the schooner, Quick picked up his grandfather and held him in his arms. At that time, the world shook. The sails of the flotilla were ripped from their mast, and in seconds, the schooner was totally gone.

Quick looked down and saw Captain Drake break into a tremendous smile. He reached out and squeezed Quick's arm and said, "I love you, Quick." He then died in Quick's arms.

Quick controlled his emotions, raised the sail, and moved off into a secluded cove. There, Quick cut up the sail and sewed it around Captain Drake's body, then attached the anchor. Taking the two long oars, Quick set out to sea as Captain Drake wished. When out of sight of land, Quick eased Captain Drake's body overboard, holding him for a moment, and said, "I love you too, Grandfather."

He then let him go and eased the anchor overboard.

CHAPTER 9:
TURMOIL

Quick returned to Galveston and set up an account to maintain the house and pay Nez's salary. He instructed her not to divulge any information about anything or to anyone except Jo Ling and his crew. Quick checked and cleaned his weapons. He destroyed all information about his wealth, except vital information he needed to access it. This, he sewed into the lining of his coat. He also sewed twenty-dollar gold pieces into the waist lining of his trousers.

Quick wanted out of Galveston as soon as possible to avoid any confrontation for the schooner being destroyed. He hurriedly packed his two saddlebags with the sewing kit, telescope, jerky, salt, and ammunition.

He hugged Nez and left with his saddlebags, the Henry, and bedroll to get Echo. Before he reached the bottom of the stairs leading to the street, he was confronted by two large men in black suits who identified themselves as Pinkerton agents representing the US government. The men were looking for Captain Drake.

The Pinkerton agents had a warrant for his arrest for destroying government property. Quick bit his tongue and said he could not help them. They thought it best for Quick to come with them since he was coming out of Captain Drake's home. They wanted a tour of the house. Wanting to stay out of trouble, Quick led them up to the door.

Nez let them in, and Quick led them through the house. Captain Drake not being there upset the Pinkerton agents. They demanded that Nez tell them where the captain was hiding. Quick dismissed Nez from their presence and said to them that if they had any questions concerning the captain, they could ask him. One of the agents reached out in a fury and grabbed Quick by the arm. "You already told us you could not help us. I'll just beat it out of you."

Quick stepped forward with his left foot going between the agent's legs. His next step was with his right foot going forward, and then his left knee slammed upward into the agent's testicles. As the agent bent forward, bellowing and reaching back between his legs, Quick's elbow struck him behind the neck, driving him to the floor and rendering him unconscious.

Throughout this time, Quick's attention had been on the other agent, forming a plan if the agent went after a gun, which he did. Not wanting to fire a shot, as the Pinkerton's gun cleared leather, the heavy bowie knife flew out of Quick's left hand, hitting the man's hand that held the gun with the heavy end of the knife's handle. Taking another step forward, Quick brought his right forearm down on the side of that agent's neck, knocking him unconscious. Quick then replaced his knife.

Quick called for Nez, telling her to straighten up the house and to send someone for a doctor. If anyone asked, tell them the agents fell down the stairs out front where he would leave them.

Quick saddled Echo and left Galveston. Everything had happened so fast in the last forty-eight hours that he had no time to plan or decide what he wanted to do. He was seventeen years old, rich, had no family, and was alone for the first time in his life.

Quick stayed off the main trail that led to Houston. Most of the old-timers and all the sea-ferrying trade called it Harrisburg, a world-class inland port. He had been close to Harrisburg many times when he was on his way to Nez's village but always dodged it to stay away from possible trouble. He decided to go into Harrisburg and would never again dodge anything or anyone because of possible trouble.

As he entered Harrisburg, Quick took a ferry over to the San Jacinto battlefield where General Sam Houston's small army chanting "Remember the Alamo" defeated Santa Anna and his much larger army. Quick had read of the battle and wanted to see the hallowed grounds. Quick was inspired by the bravery of Sam Houston and his men and wished he might have had a part in the battle. After seeing the battleground, it made him even more proud to be a Texan.

Quick was aware of the gawks and stares he received but did not let it bother him. This was not uncommon, especially since he started wearing the two Colts and carrying the Henry. Most everyone was armed, but not as well as Quick.

Quick left Echo in a livery with plenty of oats and water, checked his weapons, and then checked himself into a hotel. Quick was mentally exhausted and wanted sleep. After eating a fast meal in the hotel café, he returned upstairs and went to bed. During the night, he planned what he wanted to do.

Quick was going to go west to see New Mexico, Colorado, Arizona, Nevada, and California. He had never been there but had studied them so long that he wanted to see if they were as he thought.

Before leaving the area, he wanted to go to Cut and Shoot and find his parents' graves. Even though he had never known them, they were his parents, and he needed to hold on to them.

By early morning, Quick was well-rested and refreshed. He carried his saddlebags, Henry, and bedroll downstairs to eat breakfast and then headed out to the livery. Quick noticed two rough-looking characters had taken an interest in him.

Echo was in high spirits and eager for the trail. Quick checked his weapons and saddled up. He then eased the Henry in his saddle scabbard. Quick left, giving no clue that he had the two thugs pegged. The two were just swinging into their saddles as he passed.

Quick knew they would try to jump him just out of earshot of town. On the outskirts of Harrisburg, Quick headed north with a steady gallop. When he found the perfect place, he rode past several yards and came back on a looping trail. He had waited ten minutes, in hidden cover, until they rode past. Quick let them get ten yards ahead, then signaled Echo into action.

Echo rushed up behind the two. Startled, the two wheeled their mounts, facing Quick and reaching for iron. Quick started pulling iron at the same time, and they knew he had them beat. They had not cleared leather and were looking down at the barrel of two Colts. They both pushed their guns back into the leather and raised their hands. Quick put his two Colts back in place. He asked why they had drawn on him. They stammered around and asked Quick what he wanted.

"Since you two were following me, I just wanted to see where you were going. I usually kill people that draw on me, and I still might. I'll ask again, why did you draw on me?"

All this time, the thugs had been backing up and spreading out. They had been lowering their hands since Quick had put his Colts back in place. Now their hands were inching toward the butts of their guns.

"Do you boys want to get killed?" No sooner than the words had left his mouth, the two thugs were again looking down the barrel of Quick's Colts. Their hands flew back in the air. The draw was so fast that they had never actually seen it. Quick put his Colts back in place and told them, "The next time I have to draw on you, you will be dead. If you want to die, reach for your guns."

"What do you want us to do?" said one of the thugs.

"I want you to ride slowly back to Harrisburg and don't look back. If I ever see you on my trail again, I will kill you. No questions asked. Do you both understand? What will it be?"

"We will ride back to Harrisburg and never get on your trail again."

"Then ride," said Quick.

Quick continued north toward Cut and Shoot, stopping every few miles to check his back trail. Toward late afternoon, Quick sought a campsite. He again wanted a good night's sleep and would continue early the next morning. His plan was to get to Cut and Shoot before dark the next day. Early the next day, Quick cut a trail that he had ridden many times; it led to Nez's village, which was east of Cut and Shoot. He decided to go there and visit his many friends, even if it meant wrestling Big Lobo.

He loved speaking the Cherokee language and listening to stories. The Cherokee were like family. He went on the lookout for game. He wanted a deer but settled for a large boar hog. It was not his favorite, but the Indians loved the strong-tasting meat.

Quick gutted the hog and built a travois to carry it to the village. He arrived in the village well before dark. Everyone was glad to see him, especially with the large boar hog. The women came forth and took the hog and prepared it for a feast.

The Cherokee took every occasion to celebrate their lives. Quick asked about Lobo and found he had gone to a northeast Cherokee village to trade furs for corn. This was good. He would not have to fake a loss to Lobo because Quick did not have the heart to defeat his friend again.

Quick brought everyone up to date on Nez and Captain Drake, leaving out all the violence. They all had a lot of respect for Captain Drake. Nez had always spoken well of him.

Quick told them of his plan to go to Cut and Shoot and find his mother's and father's gravesite, then go on a trek to California. The next morning, they saw Quick off and wished him well on his journey.

CHAPTER 10:
THE CUT AND
SHOOT KILLINGS

Early the next morning, Quick stopped at the livery in Cut and Shoot and asked the hostler where the cemetery was located.

"The name's Rainey. Don't think I know you, young feller. Who are you looking for there?"

"Pete and Abby Gale Tender," Quick replied.

A shocked look appeared on Rainey's face that he could not hide.

"You be kin?" Rainey asked.

"Father and mother," Quick replied.

Rainey hurriedly told Quick how to get to the cemetery. Rainey was eyeing the two Colt .45s and the Henry rifle with wonderment. That being, could Quick use them, or were they for show?

"Didn't know Pete had a son as old as you," said Rainey.

"I'm his only son."

Quick thanked Rainey for the directions, and he turned toward the cemetery. Out of the corner of his eye, Quick saw Rainey, who was stooped and old, move out as spry as a young rooster. The excitement in his movement told Quick that he could hardly wait to tell someone something. Why would his desire to go to his parents' gravesite be of interest to anyone?

Rainey could hardly wait to spread the news. He sought out Melvin and Christy Cole and told them Pete Tender's son was in town, packing iron and on the prod. Rainey told them that Tender was going to the cemetery.

Melvin and Christy decided it best to look him up before he looked them up. They determined that Quick was seventeen years old and packing that much iron meant that he was probably going to try to kill them. They agreed to just go ahead and kill him, then claim self-defense. They told Rainey to look up Brandon Cole. Tell him that Pete Tender's son was in town hunting them. They rode to the cemetery to confront Quick.

Quick had just arrived and dismounted. When he saw the two riders racing up and coming to an abrupt halt about ten yards from him, Quick signaled Echo to move aside.

"We understand you've come looking for us," Melvin barked.

"I don't know you."

"Well, I'm Melvin Cole, and this is my brother Christy." Quick replied, "So!"

"We killed your father."

"I'm not looking for you, and I want no trouble," replied Quick.

"We know you are only seventeen years old, and that's mighty young for you to die, but we don't want to get bushwhacked, or you to grow up thinking you can use those guns. Now you are armed, and we are going to kill you in self-defense, right here in the open. We will give you a chance to go for your gun first."

Quick knew he had to kill them but wanted it to be fair. Quick did not want them to think this was going to be easy, and he wanted to put some doubt in their minds.

"What makes you think you can outdraw me?" Quick asked. Melvin answered, "Well, there's two of us," as he smiled.

"Well, I have two guns, and I can fire both at the same time."

Quick smiled. "You had better start grabbing your iron first." Quick moved two steps to his left as Melvin and Christy reached for their guns. Everything seemed to be in slow motion for Quick. Their guns had not cleared leather before his left hand reached for the Colt in his belt as the right hand came up over his left, with both guns firing at the same time. Melvin's and Christy's lives ended with a .45 slug that was shot squarely between each of their eyes.

Quick replaced the spent shells and returned the Colts to their proper place. He had stayed calm through his first and hopefully last gun battle. He had concentrated and anticipated every move that the Cole brothers would take. He felt no remorse. It was a life-or-death situation, and he would move on as Jo Ling told him to do.

Quick loaded and tied the Cole brothers on their horses and headed back to Cut and Shoot to tell the sheriff what happened.

The word had spread that Pete Tender's son had returned and was looking for the Cole brothers. As Quick re-entered the town, excited people came from all directions. It was evident that a majority were glad the Cole brothers were dead. There were smiles, slaps on the back, and a look of glee on many faces.

Quick did not know what brought on this response other than they did not like the Cole brothers. A lot of talk focused on how this kid could kill the Cole brothers, who were tough and had notches on their guns. Many were glad the two were dead but speculated that the kid had to have bushwhacked them. Quick was being asked about what had happened.

Quick had learned from Jo Ling to never give an explanation to a mob, regardless if they were a friendly mob or not. Quick diverted the questions by asking the whereabouts of the sheriff. The mob that had gathered around Quick and the bodies of the Cole brothers parted as the sheriff and Rainey rode up.

Sheriff Brandon Cole went straight to the bodies tied to their horses. He saw the hole between each of their eyes, then turned, with his pistol pointing straight at Quick, and announced he was under arrest for murder.

Brandon's deputy, Jake Lyons, had just arrived on the scene and was ordered to disarm the prisoner and cuff him. As Jake disarmed Quick and began cuffing him, Quick had already picked the key to the cuff from Jake's pocket.

Brandon instructed the undertaker to take the bodies and prepare them for burial and to send their horses to the livery. Brandon took the two Colts and pulled the Henry from its scabbard.

Brandon wanted Quick's horse taken to the jail, so his saddlebags and bedroll could be searched.

The crowd followed the sheriff, Quick, and the deputy to the jail. Quick had not spoken a word about the killings. He turned as he reached the door of the jail and shouted for all to hear that he could explain this to the satisfaction of the sheriff and would be free shortly.

Quick had shown no resistance to being arrested. Sheriff Cole grabbed Quick by the arm and led him into the jailhouse. He seated Quick in a straight-back chair across from him. Quick eased the key into the lock of the left-hand cuff and, while loudly coughing, turned the key, and then moved the key to the right cuff.

Sheriff Cole told Quick that with the evidence he had, it would be a speedy trial. He would schedule the hanging four days after the trial. He said he wanted to give all the spectators time to get to Cut and Shoot and spend their money.

The sheriff was fascinated with the Henry; it was the first one he had seen. He told Jake to go out, remove the scabbard from Quick's horse, and put it on his saddle. He told Quick that he was

confiscating his Colts and the Henry because he was sure Quick had stolen them.

Quick made no effort to communicate with the sheriff but asked to speak with the judge. He told Quick he would see the judge soon enough. The judge would be eager to speak with him since the judge was the Cole brothers' first cousin. "If you have anything to say, say it to me," said the sheriff.

Quick then spoke up and told the sheriff that he was not going to sit by and be railroaded for killing the Cole brothers when it was in self-defense. The sheriff laughed and told him to tell him about the self-defense.

Quick told him he tried to talk them into not drawing on him. "They did, and it was either kill or be killed. They drew first, and I killed them."

Brandon let out a loud rebuttal. "You expect me to believe you shot them both before they got off a single shot?"

"I had two guns," replied Quick.

"You had to have bushwhacked them. Melvin and Christy were faster with their guns than anyone in the county, and I guarantee you, we are going to hang you. I know you are young, but anyone that packs iron like you is old enough to be hanged."

Quick calmly stood up, and the sheriff stood also, drawing his gun as he moved around the desk.

"Sheriff, I don't want to hurt or kill you, but like I said, Quick continued, "I'm not going to sit around and let you hang me."

Quick flipped off the cuffs as the sheriff was raising his gun to slap Quick up beside the head. Quick reached out with his left hand, slid his finger behind the trigger to prevent it from firing, and released a chopping blow to the lower neck of the sheriff. The sheriff folded like an accordion. Quick held the gun with his finger behind the trigger all the way to the floor. He then removed it from the sheriff's hand, unloaded the cylinders, and pitched the gun into the wastebasket.

Quick picked the sheriff up and put him in his chair. Quick retrieved his Colts, slid his belly-gun in place, threw his holster in place, and then checked the action and ammunition of both. He then reached for the Henry. After checking it, he sat down, facing the sheriff and the door.

When Jake reentered, Quick stood, fully armed, but made no sign of hostility. Quick made no effort to disarm Jake, knowing there would be little danger if he did try to arrest him, and it would make it easier for him to ask for his help. Jake made no effort to challenge Quick. Quick told Jake exactly what had happened with the Cole brothers and what the sheriff told him. He told him what he did to the sheriff. Quick asked Jake to share his side of the killings with the community and the Texas Rangers, who he would be contacting as soon as possible.

Quick asked Jake to help move the sheriff to the nearest cell. Quick mentioned that he did not want to get him in trouble with the sheriff or judge and suggested it might be best that he takes his gun and lock him up with the sheriff. A relieved expression crossed Jake's face, and he agreed. Quick told Jake he would stay until the sheriff regained consciousness, and then he would place a gag in their mouths and tie their hands and feet. Quick suggested that when they were free, to let the sheriff do all the explaining. He promised Jake he would return as soon as possible to clear his name.

When leaving, Quick locked the cell door and put the key in his pocket. The crowd had dispersed by the time Quick left. He placed the "Be Back Soon" sign on the front door, then locked the door and took the key.

Quick retrieved his rifle scabbard from the sheriff 's saddle and rode out of town, calmly returning waves as he went. Quick rode east out of town and then cut north to loop back toward the graveyard. He stopped and walked back to cover his trail. He picked a bouquet of wild roses then proceeded to the cemetery.

It took only a few minutes to locate the gravestones. In silence and deep thought, Quick placed the flowers on his mother's grave, kissed his fingers and reached down, and touched the grave. He then kneeled to the ground and placed his hand on his father's grave, and a tear fell from his cheek.

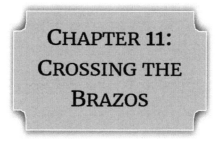

CHAPTER 11:
CROSSING THE
BRAZOS

Quick was not concerned with killing the Cole brothers. It was kill or be killed. His conscience was clear on that. After seeing the town's response, he knew they needed killing. All he needed now was time to clear his name.

His concern was to stay free until he could get a fair trial. He felt the only way to do that was to contact the Texas Rangers. He knew the sheriff would be on his trail, and he would need to fake them out. The posse would give out in a couple of days and lose their enthusiasm. All that would be left would be kinfolks, which were always dangerous.

He had nothing to keep him in Texas and had initially decided to go to California. So that is where he would go. He would head toward Mexico, leaving a clear trail to follow. He would lose the posse and head northwest, then go west to California. As soon as he had time, he would write a letter to the Texas Rangers.

Quick had lost the posse and was now heading to Washington on the Brazos. He planned to take the ferry across the Brazos. Quick thought the ferry was a good choice rather than trying to cross the sandy, steep-banked Brazos elsewhere.

After eight days of cautious, leisurely riding, Quick arrived just at dusk. The ferry was closed for the night. There were several cabins constructed mostly with hand-hewn boards of mostly cottonwood and pecan.

Washington on the Brazos was the site of the provisional government of the Republic of Texas. They met there on March 1, 1836 and signed the Declaration of Independence from Mexico on March 2, 1836. It was now the primary crossing site of the treacherous Brazos River for many miles.

Mostly Mexican families lived there. Many in their family fought with the Texans for their independence from Mexico. Families were cooking their meals outdoors to escape the sweltering heat indoors.

Quick spotted a lone man starting a fire. Quick, in perfect Spanish, asked, "Can you tell me when the ferry will be in service?"

Laughing, he responded with, "It is when the ferry owner has the notion, señor, and he is not always notional but can be influenced with money."

He asked Quick to join him for coffee. After thanking the man, Quick dismounted and threw the reins over the saddle, letting Echo free to graze.

He complimented Quick on his perfect Spanish language and stated he was trying to learn English. He said he was trying to read anything he could find written in English. He then pulled out an Austin Gazette that he had picked up four days previously. He said he tried to read it all the way home from Austin, but it was very confusing.

It took all the training Quick had done to hold his composure. The headline read, "Two Deputy Sheriffs Murdered in Cut and Shoot by Quick Tender." The article went on to say:

Quick Tender was a bloodthirsty killer with a history of evil doings. Tender bushwhacked the deputies, who were hot on his trail for murder, the theft of two .45 Colt revolvers, and a government-issue .44 Henry repeating rifle. Sheriff Brandon Cole had captured

Tender and had him secure in jail, where his gang broke in and overpowered the sheriff and his jailer, Jake Lyons. It is thought that there were six in the gang, five inside and one held the horses. The sheriff placed a reward of $1,000, dead or alive, on Tender and any of his gang. The sheriff cautioned that Tender was extremely dangerous and should be shot on site. Sheriff Brandon Cole estimated that Tender had been involved in ten murders and numerous thefts. The sheriff said Tender was around twenty years old, a slick dresser, and a glib talker. His location was unknown, but he was expected to be headed to Mexico. The sheriff had asked the Texas Rangers to get involved because of the murder of law enforcement officers.

Quick rode south along the Brazos for several miles and then turned northeast for about a mile. He dismounted, walked back to where he turned and wiped out all his tracks back to Echo. With the help of the stars, Quick rode north until near daylight. Locating a knoll, he dismounted and unsaddled Echo. He took his telescope, canteen, jerky, and the Henry with him as he walked toward the top of the knoll. Not wanting to skylight himself, he stayed below the top, as he eased to the west side.

He was closer to the Brazos than he thought. Through the telescope, he could see several miles in all directions, except east, from where he sat. He would check that direction shortly. The Brazos was less than a mile to his west. Quick searched for low banks on both sides of the river for possible crossing sites. The Brazos was well known for its swiftness and sandy crumbling banks, which created large areas of quicksand. Captain Drake had told Quick numerous times about their danger. There would never be a safe, low exit point directly across from a low entry point. Quick had located several possibilities of places to cross.

Taking one last long look on the west side and detecting no movement or other signs to indicate danger, Quick moved slowly to the east side and continued his search of possible danger. Finding nothing, Quick eased to the bottom of the knoll.

A soft whistle for Echo brought him at once. Quick moved away from the knoll and found a suitable location to spend the day. He gave Echo a large portion of oats and watered him with his hat. He built a small fire with dry wood under thick mesquite to disperse any smoke. He made coffee and cooked a large amount of bacon on a green stick. After eating, he separated and buried all traces of a fire. He sought out a spot with the most shade, where he would now sleep out the day and cross the river well before dark. He checked his weapons and curled up in the shade around the base of a large mesquite and slept. He knew Echo would alert him of any danger.

Quick woke with the sun bearing down on him from a low angle. He estimated that it was around three o'clock. After checking his weapons, he went back to the knoll and again searched all directions for signs of danger. Quick needed a plan. But he had to get on the west side of the Brazos, and now was the time. It was so dangerous to cross the Brazos on horseback, which only fools and desperate people tried. He now fell in that category. He knew that if any horse could do it, Echo could.

Heading out to the nearest valley he had located from the knoll, Quick had hoped to be lucky. No such luck. The closest exit did not allow enough time for Echo to get across the river. Finally, Quick located a good possibility. He could enter the river where it was much wider, creating a slower river flow. He thought Echo could swim up the river against the slower current. If he could not get to the desired exit point, he could retreat to his point of entry, exit, and look for another location to cross the river.

Quick rode north to get a good look at the exit point. The exit was steeper than the entrance, but Echo was a mustang and had crossed rivers before. Quick rode Echo to the entrance, held the Henry and saddlebags high above his head, and with only a small amount of coaxing, Echo entered the river. Quick turned him up the stream and across the river. When the exit neared, Quick leaned forward in the saddle and raked Echo's flanks with both heels of his boots. This was Echo's signal to race up the incline. Echo got halfway up when he started running in place, trying to stay on top of the falling sand that was caving in on all sides. There wasn't anything Quick could do but lean forward. This gave Echo just enough increase in power to let him jump ahead of the caving sand. In three leaps, he was clear of the caving sandy bank.

CHAPTER 12: ALIAS WILLIAM PEACEMAN

After finding a new place to camp on the west side of the Brazos, Quick dried and cleaned his weapons. He removed all the wet shells, put them in an old sock, and put them back in his saddlebag. He removed a pencil and paper from his saddlebag. He had to have a new name, a story, and a new outward appearance.

He hated everything about having to do this, but he had no choice. After much thought, he came up with William Peaceman. It would be easy for him and others to remember. He wrote the name fifty times. By then, he could write it with ease and exactness each time, without hesitation. He had never heard of the name before and hoped it would be one that had no relatives.

The name needed a story. He decided to be an orphan that had been left a small inheritance. He had left Tennessee at the age of twelve and had drifted down to Texas. He never stayed anywhere over a couple of weeks. He had worked odd jobs and never liked cities. He felt he could always feed himself in the country by trapping and fishing. He was now seventeen years old and very happy with his life.

When near a city, village, or trading post, he would only carry one visible Colt, that being the one behind his belt in front. It was less noticeable and less threatening than the low slung one in the holster. He would depend on his other weapons, Dillinger, knives, and body, if necessary.

Echo was a nondescript horse. There were thousands that looked like him. Even if they were not, he would not give up Echo for another.

He would break down the Henry and hide it in his bedroll and discard his saddle scabbard. When in the country, he would carry both Colts and carry his Henry in his right hand across his saddle horn, leaving his left hand free to reach for his .45 behind his belt or bowie knife on his left hip. Quick would not cut his beard and would let his hair grow until it interfered with the throwing of his knife from his neck holster.

Quick set out to tell the real story concerning the Cole brothers to the Texas Rangers. He wrote in detail about why he went to Cut and Shoot and about his talk with Rainey, the hostler. He told of the incident at the cemetery. He pointed out that the Cole brothers did not wear badges or hold themselves out as lawmen. He used the exact words that were used, where he stood, and where the Cole brothers set their mounts. He told of carrying the bodies to Sheriff Brandon Cole and about the crowd and their reactions to the deaths. He told of his conversation with the sheriff and the action he took. He told of his escape and Deputy Jake Lyons's presence, who could be a witness to the escape.

Quick said he wanted to turn himself in after the rangers did a thorough investigation. He told them that until then, he had to stay on the run and try to keep from being killed by some bounty hunter. He signed the letter and placed it in the envelope. He also placed the front page of the newspaper in with the letter, sealed, and addressed it. Texas Rangers – Austin, Texas.

Quick was sure it would get there once it was mailed. He did not like being on the run, but he knew the necessity of it. It was then that he decided to go to Fort Shirley at Flat Creek and contact Colonel Freeman.

Quick would not be in a hurry to get anywhere. He knew it would take several months after they received his letter to complete any investigation, even if they did investigate. He also realized he would not have access to his money at Wells Fargo without fear of revealing his whereabouts. He had to be careful about how he spent the money he did have.

Quick set out for Flat Creek, then decided to cut across to Salado, a major stagecoach stop on Salado Creek that emptied into the Lampasas River. Salado sat north of Austin and south of Waco. Salado had a reputation for having good food and friendly card games among layover stage passengers. Quick had comfort in knowing that he had never had a picture made of him that would be on a Wanted poster. He also felt comfortable around educated, wealthy people and those with limited knowledge and no wealth. It mattered not to him, their race, language spoken, or clothes worn. He was always comfortable around everyone and sought conversation that would make them comfortable around him.

He had never sought attention to himself. Quick knew that people loved to talk about themselves, and he never spoke about himself unless he was asked. Then he would keep it short and again, ask them a question about themselves.

He now needed to keep a lower profile but spread false information where others could hear. He had to be especially careful about what he said around lawmen. He knew that each would have a Wanted poster on him, and it would be posted around town since it had a $1,000 reward, dead or alive.

Quick needed money and supplies. He was confident he could win all the funds he needed and not draw attention if the pots he won were kept low. With all the layover passengers from the stage, it should be easy to get up a game.

CHAPTER 13: THE SALADO KILLINGS

The trip to Salado was uneventful. When he got close to Salado, the country changed to rolling hills with an abundance of game and large native pecan trees. Along the tributaries leading to Salado Creek were large cottonwoods.

Salado Creek was wide and shallow with a limestone bottom and large rock outcroppings. As the clear water rushed by the rocks, fish could be seen lurking just outside the eddy, waiting to pounce on the smaller fish that passed by. There were several large cypress trees with their protruding roots reaching out of the water. The surroundings and the water rushing past the rocks created tranquil sounds that were lulling Quick into a peaceful, complacent yet dangerous mindset. He shook his head and reminded himself he needed to be vigilant and to remind Echo to be alert.

Quick realized why the stage line company selected Salado to be their way station. The shallow rushing creek, the trees, and the game animals made people want to relax and stay awhile. The company built the hotel and restaurant to accommodate them.

After breaking down and rolling the Henry and his hip Colt in his bedroll, Quick eased into the small community around noon and placed Echo in the only public stable. Quick had observed the free-standing three-story building that backed up to the creek, with an alley on each end. The sign on the front announced Stagecoach Inn-Cafe-Saloon; on each end of the building was a door with another in the middle. On the second and third floors were windows at the end of each hall.

Quick sauntered into the hotel and asked for a room on the third floor, facing the creek. He wanted to be vigilant of people coming and going in Salado but having the best place to escape from would precede that.

When the clerk turned to the key rack to see what was available, Quick took the opportunity to look at the guest registration book. He took mental notes of names, room numbers, and dates of the registered guests.

The clerk was happy to rent a room on the third floor. The clerk mentioned most guests did not want to climb more steps than they had to, and most were afraid of fire and wanted the lowest room available. Quick said he wanted the quietness that the third floor would give him and that he was not afraid of fire. The clerk mentioned he had three rooms side by side and that Quick could have the one in the middle. When the clerk had other rooms available, he would refrain from renting the other two. He told Quick of the fire escape rope at the end of each hall, and that the rope would reach the ground. Quick wrote the name William Peaceman, as if it belonged to him, without hesitation.

When Quick reached the hallway to his room, he noticed the oak floor did not squeak; he would fix that. Loose boards do not squeak. In his room was a pitcher of water and a glass. Filling the glass, Quick returned to the hall and sprinkled the water in both directions from his door. He would check it before leaving the third floor.

Quick returned to his room, took a small mirror and a bar of soap from his saddlebag, and approached the window slowly. Pushing the curtain aside while staying in the darkened area of the room, he looked out the window, across and up and down the creek. Seeing no one, he unlatched the window, rubbed the bar of soap up and down both sides of the window casing, and then raised it. Still standing in the darkened area of the room, Quick hooded the mirror from the sun, reached out to see the reflection of the ground, then up and down the back wall. He then tested the windowsill, making sure it was solid and secure. Seeing no one, he lowered the window and placed the curtain back over the window.

Moving back into the hallway, he tested his remedy for the lack of squeak in the floors. Walking lightly up and down the hall created the amount of squeak he desired. He would check it each day. Quick locked his room, then removed the thin-bladed pick from the scabbard in his left boot and went to the room on his left. He inserted the thin blade and aligned the tumblers within a few seconds. He entered the room, unlatched the window, and applied the soap on the casing, raising it up and down several times. He left the window open and tested the sill. It, too, was solid and sound. He left the room and repeated the process on the room to the right of his but latched the window.

Quick returned to his room, locked the door, and placed a chair under the knob. Quick removed five twenty-dollar gold pieces from his waistband, put them in his pocket, and then checked his weapons. He was leaving one of his Colts behind with his Henry. Quick, not wanting his saddlebags, Colt, and Henry stole or searched, now felt comfortable that his room could not be broken into easily. Quick opened his window, again looking outside with the help of his mirror, and then hung on to his windowsill. He reached out with one hand and closed the window. He retrieved his thin pick from his left boot and latched the window. He eased over to the corner of the windowsill, swung to the left, then right; picking up speed, he lunged for the open window in the room next door and pulled himself into the room with ease. He lowered the window and locked it, then went to the door, listened a few minutes, then entered the hall, locking the door behind him.

After checking his weapons, Quick walked down the stairs to the lobby. Two guests looked up, acknowledging him with a nod. Quick did the same as he passed on the way to the dining room on his right. Upon entering, he located five people in the room, without looking directly at them. He chose a table near the rear and in the middle, where he could see each of them with a slight turn of his head. Here, he would be able to hear more conversation and have more avenues of escape, if needed. He planned and saw how he could get to any attacker with a thrown knife, if necessary. He was relaxed, calm, and had a slight smile on his face. He could hear conversations without turning and looking.

The waitress arrived with a glass of water and asked if he would be having coffee.

"Yes, and I'm hungry, so what you have available is fine with me," replied Quick.

She returned with a huge steak, green beans, boiled potatoes, and a large plate of sliced tomatoes. The tomatoes were gone before the steak, and another dish arrived without having to ask.

After the meal was finished, the waitress asked, "Apple or cherry pie?"

"Both."

After eating the two pieces of pie, Quick sat, enjoying his third cup of coffee. The waitress returned to the table. "I sure like to see a man eat when he's hungry. They had no food from where you came?"

Quick took the opportunity to start spinning his story. Speaking loud enough that people interested in hearing could. He said he came out of Tennessee, taking odd jobs, through Arkansas. He ate well until he got lost after he crossed the Sulphur River. He told her he had sufficient money to buy food but could not find anyone that had enough to sell. He said he crossed the Sabine, thinking it was the Trinity. He stayed on the Sabine a few days and ate plenty of fish he caught in a trap. He stated that he was not a good enough shot to kill any game. After leaving the Sabine, he found a camp that shared their evening meal and the information that he had not crossed the Trinity, but the Sabine instead. He told her that he had not had a map and knew little about geography. He only knew what he was told by others along the way. Laughing, he told her he had eaten a lot of bird eggs along the way getting here.

"Where you headed?" she asked.

"Nowhere in particular," Quick responded. "Just want to work my way south to see the Gulf of Mexico."

There were whispers in the room. Quick could not hear most of them, but he did hear the word greenhorn. Good, Quick thought.

Quick paid his bill of fifty cents and went across the hotel lobby to the saloon. He was sized up by the twelve people in the room, including the barkeeper. To show no weakness, Quick returned their stares. He casually walked to the far end of the bar and ordered a beer. It took no time to locate the door that led to the alley. It was behind a partition, behind the bar with only an open passageway. The only other entry or exit was the swinging door he had just entered.

There were two card games being played. Quick determined one was for the regulars that had no desire for outside players and the other a full table, high-stakes game. Quick needed to replenish his supplies and bankroll but did not want to start off in a high-stakes game. It was not that he could not win, but he did not want the attention.

Three of the men from the dining room joined Quick at the bar. After ordering their drinks and a few minutes of casual conversation, their leader, a big six-feet-two-inch, 280-pound rough and slick man, introduced himself to Quick. "Name's Haskell, and this is Bo and Sid."

"My name is William Peaceman," said Quick.

Haskell told Quick that they were just killing time waiting on the stage to Dallas, which would not arrive until ten o'clock the next morning. Haskell asked Quick if he would like to join them for a friendly game of poker. Quick told them that he liked poker and would like to play. The gleam in their eyes signaled Quick that they had found their mark. The game started with a low ante of $1 and pot limit. Quick won several small hands, expressing glee each time. It was suggested that the ante be raised to $5. Quick played his mark role and agreed.

Haskell was the mechanic, and Bo and Sid were just shills. They were there just to build up the pot. Haskell had been dropping hands from the bottom of the deck, dealing seconds, and from the bottom of the deck. He was directing the shills as to what to do with hand signals. Quick had played for an hour holding his own, then losing several large hands. Now he had everyone, and everything figured out.

Quick asked that they raise the ante to $10 so he could get some of his money back. They all agreed. Again, he saw the glee in their eyes. Quick had won several small hands with the higher ante. During these hands, Haskell dealt the cards. Haskell had signaled Bo and Sid to fold, and Haskell would fold after the first bet, letting Quick win the hand.

Quick felt now was the time to win the money on his deal. He knew Haskell was set up to make his move. Quick dealt Haskell three aces, a seven, and a nine. Haskell bet $10 and signaled Bo and Sid to just call. Quick raised $10, and Bo and Sid called, and Haskell raised another $10. Bo and Sid called, and Quick made a hesitant call.

Haskell took one card, and Quick gave him a nine. This gave Haskell a full house. Bo and Sid drew two cards each, and Quick drew one. Haskell bet $20, and Quick raised the size of the pot to $180. Bo and Sid folded. Haskell called and raised $300. Quick only called because that would halt the betting, and he would not be able to cover another large bet. Haskell gleefully turned over his ace-high full house, and Quick planned ahead as to what was going to happen when he turned over his four deuces and one ace.

Haskell, Bo, and Sid were speechless for a few seconds. Quick reached out with his right hand to pull in the pot as Haskell rose to his feet and demanded that Quick take his hand off the pot. Quick knew that Haskell would do all the fighting and that Bo and Sid would only do what they were told to do. Quick responded calmly that four deuces beat a full house as he continued stacking up the pot.

Quick did not want to bring attention to himself but spoke up loud enough to let everyone in the saloon know that he won the pot. Haskell reached out to grab Quick's hand. Rising, Quick grabbed Haskell's hand and then, turning his back to Haskell, backed up toward him, twisting his hand and arm upward over his shoulder and kicked Haskell's feet from under him. With Haskell's 280 pounds pulling down and Quick pulling down on the arm that was over his shoulder, Haskell's arm cracked like a rifle shot. Bo and Sid backed away as Haskell screamed while lying on the floor. Quick picked up his money and backed out of the saloon while everyone stared.

After checking his weapons, Quick went up the stairs and down the squeaking hallway to the room next to his. He unlocked the door, entered, and relocked the door. He opened the window, eased out and, hanging on the sill, reached up and pulled the window down. He eased over to the edge of the sill and swung out to grasp the windowsill of his room. Unlocking and pushing the window up, he eased into his room.

Now for a plan. He had not seen any lawmen, nor had he asked about any. He did not want to bring attention to himself by asking. He knew Haskell would put Bo and Sid after him. He would not run. He decided to go back to the saloon. He would explain to the bartender and everyone there that he was defending himself and did not want the altercation to turn into a shooting and hurt an innocent bystander. Leaving his room through the room next door, Quick walked down the squeaking hallway and down the stairs to the lobby. All extraordinary sounds had ceased.

Quick looked in over the batwing door and saw that all the tables and chairs had been straightened, and Haskell, Bo, and Sid were gone. He looked at everyone in the room and, seeing no threat, entered. All present looked up at him, as before, and then returned to their business. He again ordered a beer and introduced himself to the bartender and owner, Ben Upton. Quick apologized for the trouble and asked if there were any damages.

"Only the broken arm of the big fellow," he said, with a grin on his face. "It must have taken a lot of courage to face as large a man as that!"

Quick explained that when Haskell grabbed him, he had no choice. He confessed that he was not a good shot and surely did not want some innocent people hurt or killed. Quick said he did not know why Haskell was so upset. He had won most of the pots and just blew up when he lost a big one.

Quick asked if there were a doctor in town that Haskell went to. Ben said that they only had a veterinary doctor in town but was sure that was where they took him. Quick asked if he thought it was advisable to speak to the law in the area and explain what had happened. Ben laughed and said, "No! I figure that Haskell would not want anyone to know that someone your size could have broken his arm."

"That's good thinking, Ben. I'll just let it lie."

Ben also explained that the sheriff only came by once a month. It would be at least three weeks before he showed up again. He stated that the sheriff spent most of his time politicking in areas that had large populations of permanent voters and not in transient towns like Salado. He did state that they did have a jailhouse in case something bad happened. The citizens could hold someone until the sheriff showed up.

On the lookout for Haskell's crew, Quick proceeded to the mercantile store and bought all the supplies he thought Echo could carry. He carried them to the stable and visited Echo. He pulled his ears and scratched his head and belly. Echo enjoyed it all. He looked fresh and rested. Quick sought the hostler and got permission to store the two gunnysacks of goods in his tack room. Quick gave him a silver dollar for the good care he had given Echo.

Being ever observant, Quick stepped out of the stable and saw Bo and Sid mounting their horses and riding off in a hurry. The horses were loaded down with all their gear, ready to be on a long trip. Quick knew they had seen him and were taking precautions for Quick not to see or recognize them. Quick moved toward the hotel and pretended not to have seen them.

Quick returned to his room through the room next door. He removed the chair from his door and placed it in the corner to the left of the door. He then worked on a plan. He knew Haskell would be after him. He decided to leave early in the morning and move any possible trouble out on the trail, if possible. If an attempt were made tonight, he would be prepared. He put his other Colt in place and placed the Henry next to the chair. He fluffed the pillows under the blanket. Standing aside from the window, he opened the curtain to let in the bright moonlight that would be shining shortly. He moved to the chair in the corner to sleep.

Quick knew not how long he had slept but was awakened by the squeaking of the floor. He heard the windows being opened at each end of the hall and the fire escape ropes being tossed out. Quick drew both Colts and silently waited. The moonlight shining through the window put a warm glow throughout the room. He made out two distinct footsteps come to his door from different directions and hesitate. In less than six seconds, the two had unloaded their six-shooters through the door and into the empty bed. They were now reloading them. Quick remained seated and waited. Bo and Sid rushed in to find the money. Seeing the empty bed, they turned and saw two fire streaks racing upward toward them from the guns of the seated Quick Tender. He now replaced the two spent bullets.

Footsteps and excited chatter were heard by Quick. He knew he did not have to worry about Bo or Sid. He knew they were dead. He did, however, have to deal with the crowd. He called out that he was okay but asked them to seek a doctor for two men that tried to kill him.

Those that were brave enough to come forward let the rest know that there was no need to call a doctor. The crowd started asking questions, and Quick, knowing there was no law around, wanted to talk to the law.

Ben Upton had been one of the first to enter the room. It was obvious as to what had happened. Ben was the first to speak about the accuracy of the shots that killed Bo and Sid. Quick explained that he had seen Bo and Sid earlier acting suspiciously around the hotel and feared an attack. He had decided to sleep sitting in the chair in the corner. When they shot through the door, filling his bed full of bullets, he drew his Colts as they rushed in. Seeing he was not dead in the bed, they turned with both guns in each of their hands. That's when Quick pulled the trigger on both of his guns. He had no time to aim. He was lucky to hit them where he did. Quick said that he was not a good shot at all. He was just scared and knew he had to pull the trigger fast, or he would be dead. He had not convinced Ben on the "luck" part. Ben and the crowd were convinced that Mr. Peaceman had killed Bo and Sid in self-defense.

Quick packed his bedroll and saddlebags, threw the bags over his shoulder, and carried the bedroll in his left hand, with his Henry inside. He pulled Ben aside and told him he would be leaving first thing in the morning and was still going to the Gulf of Mexico. Ben told Quick that there had already been a lot of talk about who he was after the fight in the bar. Now they were really talking about the two perfect shots between the eyes of Bo and Sid. "They don't believe the story about not being a good shot and want to know who you really are."

"Tell them I'm someone that minds his own business, that wants to be left alone, and that will always defend himself."

Quick gave Ben $100, asked Ben to have someone bury Bo and Sid, and give the balance to pay for damages to the hotel. "I will feel better sleeping under the stars tonight and will be gone before the town awakens."

Ben wished Mr. Peaceman good luck and added, "I don't think you will ever need luck, though, with the way you handle yourself."

The fire escape ropes Bo and Sid had thrown out the window had not been retrieved. Catching the right movement, while everyone was in his room, Quick grabbed one of the ropes and rappelled down the side of the hotel to the ground and disappeared in the shadows and darkness.

After observing the town's movements, Quick stayed in the shadows and silently made his way to the stable. Quick signaled Echo for quietness as he saddled him. He unrolled the bedroll and assembled the Henry and slid it into the scabbard. He buckled his holster with his Colt and tied on the bedroll.

Moving to the tack room, while being quiet as to not wake the hostler, he removed the two sacks of supplies and tied them to the saddle horn and threw his saddlebags in place. He mounted Echo and moved off in the darkness, heading south toward Austin. After traveling about five miles, he turned west in a rocky draw toward Goldthwaite. He rode west for twenty minutes, then stopped, dismounted, and walked back to the main road. He shielded a match and looked for any sign he might have left. He only saw a couple of marks that could be signs then brushed them out and returned to Echo, where he mounted and continued his journey.

Quick had decided to bypass Lampasas, which was a bustling town with multiple crossing roads and trails going in all directions. It had several trading posts and saloons with gamblers, prostitutes, and cowboys. It was a straighter route to Goldthwaite, but his encounter in Salado added to the necessity of staying out of the highly traveled areas until he could put the incident in Cut and Shoot behind him.

Quick hated the position he was in but felt confident everything would work out. Little did he know that in the five days it would take to get to Goldthwaite, the noose would tighten. He had not considered the bounty hunters, and lawmen would be looking for him any place but toward Mexico. The killing of Bo and Sid had changed all that. The shot between the eyes of each man was all too familiar to the bounty hunters and lawmen. Several near Salado joined the hunt immediately. Others would arrive as soon as they could.

CHAPTER 14: THE CREW GOES TO CUT AND SHOOT

I t had been ten days since Quick had escaped from the jail in Cut and Shoot when Jo Ling read the fictitious story. It took four days to round up the crew: Fazio, Ross, Paul, and Boris. It took two full days of hard riding to arrive on the west fork of the San Jacinto River, where camp was made for the night. They were now ten miles from Cut and Shoot, and now was the time to make some plans.

The crew had virtually raised Quick. He was in deep and dangerous trouble. They did not doubt Quick's abilities, but he now faced an overwhelming force brought on by the desire for the large reward amount. He was wanted dead or alive. Increased interest would be forthcoming from every lawman in the country because, supposedly, lawmen had been killed. The crew knew Quick well enough to know that he did not have to bushwhack anyone. Regardless, they were going to back Quick, right or wrong, with each of their lives if necessary.

It was decided that each would ride into Cut and Shoot from different directions and different times. They would keep their ears to the ground and pick up any information as to what happened and where Quick might be headed.

Jo Ling wanted each of them to make visual contact with the sheriff and his horse and make mental notes of the sheriff and the horse's tracks for future reference. Early the next morning, the crew moved out to Cut and Shoot.

Boris found out the shooting took place around the cemetery, and that Quick had loaded the bodies on their horses and delivered them to the sheriff. Boris got directions to the cemetery. He then rode off in the opposite direction until he was out of sight of the one that gave him the directions. When he had ridden far out of sight, he looped around town and went to the cemetery.

Boris had easily picked up Echo's hoof prints. As a matter of fact, he found two sets. Quick had gone to the cemetery twice. Outside the cemetery gate, he found bloodstains in the dirt and other signs made when the bodies were loaded on their horses. He found Quick's boot prints leading into the cemetery and followed them to the grave markers of Pete and Abby Gale Tender.

A bouquet of wild roses that were on Abby Gale's grave was now wilted. Boris picked up on a clear track of Quick riding away to the southwest. No attempt was made to cover the track, which told Boris that he wanted everyone following him to know he was going southwest toward Mexico. Boris knew Quick's tracks would disappear down the trail, and he wanted Paul, the expert tracker in the crew, to make the determination as to where Quick was really going.

Ross had found a low-stakes poker game at the Flying Rooster Saloon, where the Cole brothers had killed Pete Tender. Ross had introduced himself to the three other players: Harold, Donny, and Vernon. His new money was welcomed. Ross managed to lose every hand, with much hoopla from the winning players. The talk was loose and casual. When mention of Quick's escape happened a second time, Ross asked what escape they were talking about.

The three eagerly expressed their opinions about the killings and escape. None thought that a gang broke Quick out of jail, but there was doubt as to how Quick shot them. None of them believed that Quick, as young as he was and how hard and fast Melvin and Christy were, could kill them both before they could get off one shot unless he had bushwhacked them. Then Vernon brought up the mystery of Quick's escape.

"How could he get out of his handcuffs and disarm Sheriff Brandon Cole and Deputy Jake Lyons, then lock them in a cell and ride casually out of town?"

Harold spoke up and gave the opinion that anyone that could do that might be capable of shooting Melvin and Christy between the eyes, in a fair fight. Vernon and Donny expressed agreement.

Ross feigned being broke and asked if he could come back tomorrow and try to win some of his money back. All expressed pleasure in that remark and welcomed him back at any time.

Paul found out that the hostler had told Melvin and Christy that Quick was on the prod for them and was heading to the cemetery.

Fazio and Paul heard that Deputy Jake Lyons had been fired that day and that Jake was afraid for his life. He had been hinting that no gang broke Quick Tender out of jail.

That night, the crew met at the rendezvous location and told of their findings. Each confirmed their visual contact with the sheriff and retained mental notes of his horse and hoof prints.

The group's opinion was that most of the townspeople were glad to be rid of Melvin and Christy and that there was no gang, just Quick Tender. In less than five minutes, it was decided that Paul Chambers, the firearms and tracking expert, would go with Boris and Fazio and track down Quick. Jo Ling and Ross would go back to Cut and Shoot and keep up with any news or developments in the situation.

Early the next morning, Paul, Boris, and Fazio moved out and picked up Quick's easy-to-follow trail. Jo Ling and Ross slipped back into Cut and Shoot from different directions.

Ross went back to the Flying Rooster. The only occupants were the bartender, Harold, and Vernon.

"Came to visit my money," said Ross.

"Welcome back. Sit down and join us for coffee," offered Harold

This was the invite he was looking for, but before he could sit or say more, the back door, behind the bar, opened.

A young man, with a frightened look on his face, was standing and motioning for someone at the table to come to him.

"Excuse me a moment," said Vernon as he rose and went to the young man.

Ross remained standing and started a casual conversation with Harold, who never took his eyes off the back door.

"Jake Lyons, Vernon's nephew. Guess he has a right to look scared," Harold said.

"How's that?" asked Ross.

"He knows no gang broke Quick Tender out of jail, and he's been talking. He had better keep his mouth shut and get out of the county, or Brandon Cole will either kill him or have him killed."

Ross saw Vernon reach in his pocket and pull out a small wad of money and give it to Jake. Jake looked down at it as Vernon patted him on the shoulder as if to apologize for the small amount and wishing he could give him more. Vernon watched Jake walk out the door. He stood for a few seconds, shaking his head and then returned to the table.

"I wanted to stop by and tell you guys how much I enjoyed the game yesterday, even though I lost every hand," said Ross.

"Sit down and have some coffee," urged Harold.

"Thanks, but I've got a long ride before me. Just got me a job running a ranch down near Victoria and can't afford to be late."

Ross shook hands with Harold and turned to do the same with Vernon, who now seemed to be a hundred miles away.

Vernon turned to Harold, "They tried to kill him last night."

"I told you so," said Harold with a wink toward Ross.

"I've got to hit the road. Thank you again for the game yesterday." Ross turned and walked out. He wanted to run at full speed. He had to find Jo Ling and get Jake Lyons to safety.

It took Ross less than five minutes to find Jo Ling and signal him to follow. In a few minutes, Ross was telling Jo Ling of Jake Lyons's plight. They agreed to find Jake and explain what they wanted: to get him to safety. They had to move fast.

It was still early in the morning, and only a few people were out and around. Jake thought that a daylight attempt on his life would not occur. The attempt last night made him know he had to get out of the county today, or Brandon Cole would succeed tonight.

Jake had little money and no plan on how to get out of the county. The bit of money his uncle Vernon had given him was not the answer. He had not collected money owed him when Brandon Cole fired him, and he was not about to ask for it. He had no idea what to do. He had been pacing up and down the alley behind the saloon since he left his uncle Vernon trying to think of something.

"Hello!" the smiling face said.

Startled, Jake fumbled at his revolver but never removed it from the holster. Ross held up both hands and said, "You don't need that. I mean you no harm and could be of help to you. I want you to take my gun from me. It will make you feel more comfortable."

"Okay, I will," Jake said.

Ross turned his holstered gun toward Jake, and while Jake was removing his gun, Ross deftly removed Jake's gun and the money Vernon had given him.

"Let's slip down to the creek and talk," said Ross. "I know of the danger you face."

"I know you. You were with Uncle Vernon in the saloon," said Jake.

"Right, I saw him give you this money," Ross said and handed it to him.

Jake reached to where he had put the money, and it was gone. "How did you get that?"

"That's not important now. I just want your total trust in me. Let's talk and let's talk about nothing but facts. If you stay here, Brandon Cole will kill you or have someone kill you tonight, right?"

"Right," said Jake.

"Another fact is that if I don't get the truth to the Texas Rangers in Austin about what happened here, Quick Tender, an innocent man, is going to get killed. He would never have a fair trial because of the lies and reward money put out by Brandon Cole."

"I don't know if he is innocent or not," said Jake.

"But you do know that no gang broke Quick Tender out of jail. You also know that Melvin and Christy were not deputies at the time they were killed and were used as such only on special occasions or when convenient to them. Isn't that a fact, Jake?"

"Yes," said Jake.

"Being an ex-law officer, don't you think everyone deserves a fair trial?" Ross asked.

"Yes," said Jake. "I liked Quick. He tried to keep me out of trouble with Brandon when he locked me up with him."

Ross told Jake of his plan to get him to Austin. He told him he wanted him to stay in the public eye and to never be alone.

Jo Ling had already found out where Jake was living. Ross wanted Jake to light all the lamps and candles before dark and for two lamps to be placed on the front porch. At 8:20 PM, he would knock slightly on the back door and wanted no light escaping from the back door when it would be opened by Jake. He would step out with nothing but the clothes he had on. Jake was to put his hand on Ross's back and follow silently.

Ross gave Jake his pistol back to him, never knowing it had been taken, and asked for his back. Jake was in awe. Ross told Jake not to mention to anyone the attempt on his life or anything concerning Quick Tender.

At 8:20 PM, Jake opened the back door. Ross led him toward the rear of a rumbling wagon. By the time the horses and the old and stooped Chinaman came into the light from the porch, Ross and Jake were securely hidden in the boxes in the rear of the wagon.

The wagon moved at a steady pace through town and eastward toward the east fork of the San Jacinto River. The Chinaman stopped and camped on the west bank of the river, waiting for daylight.

Before crossing, two riders rushed up in a cloud of dust and demanded to see the boxes. The old Chinaman feigned fear and spoke nothing but Chinese. Finding nothing but Chinese clothes, the men rushed off.

After jumping off the wagon less than a half-mile out of town and making sure all their foot tracks were well hidden, Ross and Jake made their way through the tall pines to the four staked horses. Two had packs, and the other two were saddled.

The horses were the best money could buy. They were large and had staying power. The plan was to ride hard for three hours then switch out the horses every three hours all the way to Austin.

CHAPTER 15:
PAUL, BORIS, AND FAZIO HOT ON THE TRAIL

After following Quick's trail from the graveyard, southwest toward Austin, it took a little time to pick up his trail going northwest. Paul saw that the posse had not found this trail. It would have been harder for Paul if he did not know Quick as well as he did.

Paul soon realized Quick wanted to get on the west side of the Brazos. The only way without swimming the Brazos was the ferry at Washington on the Brazos. Paul lost Quick's trail a few hundred feet from the ferry because of the heavy traffic. They got lucky as the ferry was just leaving when they rushed on.

After they made it across, they rode west for three miles and turned north to pick up Quick's trail. When the trail was not found, they turned south, going all the way back to the Brazos.

"He did not cross the river. Something must have spooked him. Let's hurry and get back across on the ferry. We need to pick up his trail before dark." Paul made loops until finally finding it. Quick had put much effort into making sure he would not be followed easily.

Quick was now looping back north to find a way to cross the Brazos. The crew had been in the same discussions with Captain

Drake about the dangers of the Brazos. Paul found the place he thought Quick had crossed. The question was, should they go back and cross on the ferry or save a day and cross now?

Taking Quick's situation into consideration, there was not one of them that would not risk giving up their life for Quick.

Paul went first, going across down the river and pulled out safely, even though he was chased out of the riverbank by falling sand behind him. He hollered for Boris to go further down the stream and take a different path out of the river. Boris had no problem getting up the bank, and it was decided that it was safe for Fazio to use the same exit.

Where was Quick headed? It was agreed with the three that he had to be going to Salado, bypassing Austin and Waco.

Their question was confirmed when they rode up on two cowboys. They had stopped to have coffee along the trail. After cautious greetings, Paul and the crew were invited for coffee. The two cowboys were coming from Abilene, going to Houston. Paul asked if they had come through Salado. An affirmative answer led to the question. "Anything going on there?"

"Nothing more than some guy by the name of William Peaceman shot two gamblers right between the eyes after they tried to kill him. They fired twenty-four shots, and he fired only two. Everyone said he told the crowd he had gotten lucky with the shots."

Paul had to put his hand over his mouth to cover the grin on his face, which soon turned to a frown. He just realized that every lawman and bounty hunter would be on Quick like stink on cow manure. Paul looked at Boris and Fazio and saw the same realization on their faces.

After thanking the cowboys for the coffee, they pushed off. Two and a half days later, they spread out and arrived in Salado.

Strangers were common in Salado, and they drew no attention. The killing of the two gamblers was still the talk of the town, and they all picked up on conversations concerning the young Mr. Peaceman. Most of the conversations were about where Mr. Peaceman had gone. Several had mentioned the coincidence of the location of the single bullet between the eyes of each of the gamblers, which was self-defense, and the same location of the two bullets in the heads of the two deputies murdered in Cut and Shoot.

The next morning, Paul and Boris were having coffee and heard a tap on the window. A very excited Fazio motioned them out. Leaving enough money on the table to pay the bill, they rushed out to join Fazio.

Fazio had just heard of a Comanche uprising near Goldthwaite. The Comanche war parties had been killing, burning, and stealing for several days when sixteen Comanche were found with a single shot between each of their eyes.

Knowing now where to head and not wanting to weigh down their horses, the group bought only ammunition and headed to Goldthwaite.

They would go through Lampasas to get to Goldthwaite and buy more provisions there. They arrived in Lampasas at sunset. It had been a hard two-and-a-half-day ride. Horses and men were beat. They would leave at noon the following day.

You don't want to go into Indian territory on spent horses. They stabled and cared for the horses, then spread out to pick up information on Indians, William Peaceman, Quick Tender, and the weather.

Lampasas intersected seven trails, five of which were well-traveled. The locals sought out people passing through. It was their way of getting information. Ninety-nine percent of the weekly paper was local news, which was already known by most.

Several local citizens expressed their opinion that it was Quick Tender that killed the two gamblers and the sixteen Comanche because that was how he killed the two deputies in Cut and Shoot.

The next day at noon, the three rode out of Lampasas on well-rested horses and with a fresh supply of provisions. The Indian situation made them slow down and be more observant. The men spread out on the trail and kept a slow but steady pace. No Indians were sighted on the way to Goldthwaite, but they did see several burned homes and barns.

Ray Stephens, owner of the trading post, looked their way as they walked in. He was helping several locals that had been burned out to replace their necessities. Several other locals were gathered around the front of the trading post visiting. Paul backed out and joined them. He casually asked about the Indian uprising. The locals were talking over themselves, telling their stories about the Comanche and their demise.

One said that cowboy Quick Tender might be a murderer, but he was a hero to them. He had single-handedly run the Comanche out of the area. It was rumored that two or three hundred of them had fled westward to San Angelo. They told of the five Indians killed on the east side of Pecan Bayou and the eleven killed south of the horseshoe curve of the Colorado.

Fazio asked if anyone met Quick Tender. One man reported that Ray Stephens had sold some supplies to a young man named William Peaceman. Mr. Peaceman turned down a request to join Stephens on his retreat to De Leon with his three Indian porters. Mr. Peaceman said he was going to cross the Colorado at the low-river crossing below the horseshoe bend of the river. This was where the Comanche were killed. Mr. Peaceman was injured by a large arrow that went through his upper thigh. He was found by Mr. Stephens' porters. Peaceman was recovering from his wound and told the porters that he had found a hideout and had been there with chills and fever. Peaceman knew he had passed out several times and knew nothing of the Indians being killed. If that wasn't Quick Tender, no one saw him.

After buying supplies from Mr. Stephens, Paul convinced him they were friends of William Peaceman and needed to find him. Paul told him he did not want Peaceman caught up in the rumors that he might be this Quick Tender.

Mr. Stephens let his porters lead Paul to where they found the wounded Mr. Peaceman. Just before the Indians left, they asked that they leave no trail to or from the hideout because they might need it themselves, especially if the Comanche returned.

The three eased up the trail and followed it to the hideout. The water hole was full of fresh water. With the river close by, it had no particular importance to wildlife. It did pick up hoofprints of a mustang in and around the dug hole. They were those of Echo. It was all the evidence needed that Mr. Peaceman was none other than Quick Tender.

While examining the rim, Fazio found a buried pile of .44-caliber spent cartridges that had been buried with four inches of gravel. The reason it was found, Fazio had asked himself a question. Where would Quick have had his lookout to shoot the Indians that would have been below? He selected the sight and laid down to get the same view that Quick would have had and accidentally uncovered the spent cartridges. The spent cartridges fit the .44-caliber Henry that Quick carried. He counted eleven!

CHAPTER 16: TEXAS RANGER MEETING

On the sixth day on the trail, Austin was in sight. It had gone well except on the fourth day out, two riders attempted to steal their horses while a third tried to hold Ross and Jake at bay.

It didn't work out for the thieves with Ross killing all three before Jake could get his gun out of the holster.

Ross explained to Jake that without their horses, the thieves could have been killing them. Ross had no remorse.

"It was self-defense. Anyway, you are supposed to hang horse thieves, and we did not have time for that," Ross explained further.

When Ross and Jake arrived at the Texas Rangers Headquarters, Ross explained that he needed to speak with Captain Smithhart, the name Quick Tender got immediate attention and excitement from Captain Smithhart's orderly. He asked Ross to sit tight and said he was sure he would be able to get him in for a meeting. Within ten minutes, Ross and Jake were escorted in to meet with Captain Randell Smithhart of the Texas Rangers and an undercover Texas Ranger by the name of Luke Shaw.

Captain Smithhart was eager to hear about this Quick Tender, mainly because it involved Sheriff Brandon Cole. Brandon Cole had been in his sight for some time. He had never pursued an inquiry because charges had never been filed against him, but rumors persisted.

Ross explained Quick Tender's background and his own involvement with Quick's grandfather. He summed up his position as law enforcement on the schooner. He told of Quick's father being killed by the Cole brothers.

Ross pointed out the training Quick received on board the schooner and why. He told of Quick's shooting abilities and the feats he performed while swinging from the mast of the schooner. Ross continued by pointing out that Quick had never been in trouble and was well tutored in minding his own business. Now, with the death of his grandfather, Quick had no family but had adequate wealth and had no animosity toward anyone. He never once mentioned Melvin's or Christy Cole's names.

Ross then had Jake tell Captain Smithhart everything he knew about the shootings, Quick bringing in the bodies, Brandon Cole's threat to hang Quick, and the escape. Then Jake told about the Cole brothers not being deputies. He told of the attempt on his own life. He told of the town's pleasure that Melvin and Christy were no longer with them.

Ross asked the captain if Jake could stay in protective custody until this could be cleared up.

"Certainly," the captain replied.

Ross handed Captain Smithhart five twenty-dollar gold pieces. "This should feed him," Ross said.

Captain Smithhart told Ross that he had never received a report from Sheriff Brandon Cole. He found out about the Cut and Shoot killings from the local newspaper. Smithhart had been suspicious of the newspaper report and wondered about not receiving a report directly from Brandon Cole. He felt the reason was that Brandon Cole did not want the Texas Rangers involved.

Smithhart explained to Ross that he had his orderly search for any reports concerning Quick Tender, and he had found none. He knew no one could commit as many crimes in Texas as the news release stated, and the Texas Rangers did not know of them.

"Ross, Luke will be on his way to Cut and Shoot shortly. Don't want the two of you traveling there together, but keep an eye out for each other," Captain Smithhart said.

"I'll be hanging out at the Flying Rooster saloon in Cut and Shoot if you need me. Mr. Shaw, I'll remember that you will be undercover."

Caption Smithhart asked Luke if he ever heard of someone bushwhacking anyone and taking the body to the sheriff.

"No," Luke said. "Unless he was a bounty hunter."

"Luke, let's not let Quick Tender get killed on a liar's word. You know the situation and the urgency. Get there as soon as possible. Luke, handle this any way you want. You know I'll back you up."

Luke Shaw was pushing thirty years of age. He was a strong broad-shouldered man. Not only strong of muscle but of brains also. He did not talk a lot, but when he did, it was all business. He was direct in his questions and demanded a straightforward answer. He lived by one law. Right is right, and wrong is wrong. It mattered not what the law said if he thought you were right; you had 100 percent of his support. It mattered not if you were a preacher, lawman, cowboy, or the town drunk. When he proved to himself that you were wrong, especially a lawman, you would feel the immediate wrath of Luke Shaw. Demanding, outspoken, and deadly. No backing down and no arguing.

CHAPTER 17:
TEXAS RANGER
LUKE SHAW'S
INVESTIGATION

Luke arrived in Cut and Shoot thinking Quick Tender was right in killing Melvin and Christy Cole. Now he was looking for the proof. He had stopped at the graveyard on the way into Cut and Shoot. He found the two stained areas of blood where the Cole brothers had fallen.

Luke visualized where Quick might have been standing when he shot them. He walked to that area and turned facing the bloodstains. He looked off in the distance and located the nearest cover, which was a group of pine trees sixty feet away. He saw the roughed-up ground where the bodies were loaded on the horses. He looked on the ground around his feet and saw nothing. He started forward and froze for over a minute. At his feet was a small round circle the size of a pencil. He looked around in all directions before bending over and gently brushing off the top dirt. A thin colored ring appeared. Digging deeper, he removed a .45-caliber casing. Standing, he slipped it in his pocket. After looking around again, he bent over and, within thirty seconds, located the second casing. He found no others. "You can't bushwhack anyone twenty feet in front of you!" Luke thought to himself.

When Luke arrived in Cut and Shoot, he knew exactly what he would do. He had thought he might have to spend a week or two on this. But now, as early as it was in the day, he planned to finish up today. He would go ahead and write up a confession for Rainey. Then, he would need Ross's assistance and would look for him in the Flying Rooster.

It was early in the morning, and coffee was still being served. When Luke entered, he sat down at a table in earshot of the only other occupied table. Ross had his back to him telling a story. The other two had turned their heads toward Luke. Luke nodded at the two as Ross turned his head also. Ross continued his story about being too late getting to Victoria to get the foreman job.

After Luke finished his coffee, he stood up, saying, "Mister, couldn't help from hearing part of your conversation. Looks as if you're unemployed. I have a friend around Austin looking for a foreman, got his address in my saddlebag if you would like to have it."

"Sure would, was just leaving now anyway," said Ross.

Ross stood by Luke as he dug aimlessly in his saddlebag. Luke pulled out a Texas Rangers' badge. Luke gave Ross several instructions to follow.

"Put this on when you need it. I need your help," Luke said in a low voice. "I want you to keep a lid on the Western Union. I need to expose myself as a Texas Ranger, and I can't have the operator contacting anyone until after I have finished with the sheriff. I'll explain as we go."

Luke continued, "When we get into the Western Union office, I will have you pin on your badge. I have one person to see and a few documents to prepare before I contact the sheriff. This could take a couple of hours. If he shows up at the Western Union before I'm ready, arrest him and hold him there."

Ross followed Luke into the Western Union telegraph office as both put on their badges. Luke had instructed Ross to lock the door and pull down the shades. The operator turned and was startled as Luke introduced himself and Ross.

The operator introduced himself as Sam Whitte. Luke extended his right hand. While shaking the operator's hand, Luke reached out and grasped the operator's shoulder.

"Sam, look at me straight in the eye. I'm going to tell you this only once. Officer Ross is my assistant. You have in your possession copies of wires you sent to most newspapers and law enforcement officers in the state concerning the killing of Melvin and Christy Cole," instructed Luke. "You are going to shut down the telegraph now and dig out all these wires. You will make a detailed list as to whom they were sent. You will give Officer Ross the copies of the telegraphs."

"I can't do that! The sheriff sent those messages!" Sam exclaimed.

"I'll take care of the sheriff, and you will do as I say!" Luke reinforced.

"The telegraph has to stay open! I can't shut it down!" refuted Sam.

"If the lines were down, you couldn't send messages, now could you?" asked Luke.

"No!" pleaded Sam.

Luke released Sam's right hand, pulled out a large knife, and cut the telegraph wire.

"That takes care of that, now go to work," ordered Luke.

"Brandon Cole will be by later to send updated telegraphs to everyone that received one before. Officer Ross, if Sam tries to contact the sheriff or tries to fix the telegraph, just go ahead and shoot him because he would be breaking the law."

"I will not break the law and I will get the list ready," the shaken Sam Whitte confirmed.

Leaving Whitte to compile the list, Luke, having already located the livery, made a beeline to it. Upon entering, he headed directly to the office inside.

"You Rainey?" Luke asked.

"Yew, sho' am," Rainey confirmed.

"Rainey, I'm Texas Ranger Luke Shaw," Luke stated as he flashed his badge. "I want to clarify a lie you told. I have two questions I will ask, and I will ask them one time. I want a truthful answer because I am not going to argue with you. Understand?"

Rainey felt as if the ranger's eyes were shooting through him as he eased out, "Shure."

"Did you tell the Cole brothers and others that Quick Tender said he was on the prod for them?" asked Luke.

"Uh, yes," Rainey stated.

"That was a lie, wasn't it?" asked Luke.

"Uh, yes," said Rainey.

"OK, Rainey, sign this confession that you lied. Your lie might get a man, Quick Tender, killed. I'm going to arrest you," explained Luke. "Right now, you are to go to the Western Union office and tap on the door lightly. Tell Texas Ranger Ross you are under arrest and that you are to stay in his custody until I release you. You are to talk to no one. I will watch you until I see you enter the telegraph office. I will release you sometime today for telling me the truth. If Quick Tender is killed because of your lie, I will be coming for you."

After Rainey entered the telegraph office, Luke went into Rainey's office and pulled out clean pages of paper and started writing. It took Luke about an hour to put everything in writing. When he was finished, he headed to the Sheriff's Office.

When Luke reached the Sheriff's Office door, he pinned on his badge and walked in. The startled sheriff and his two deputies were reaching for their guns before realizing the man standing in the doorway not only had a Texas Rangers' badge on but also had two Colt .45s pulled and pointing straight at Sheriff Brandon Cole. Sheriff Cole put out his hands, palms down on the desk, and shouted for everyone to settle down.

"Sheriff, I'm Texas Ranger Luke Shaw. I have a problem, and you have a bigger one. I come here to discuss my problem with you. So that no one gets killed, I'm going to take all your guns and place your two deputies in a cell. Then, since I don't think you would want your deputies to hear what I will say, I'll close the door."

There was no doubt who had the authority in the room. Not because of the badge of a Texas Ranger or him having the only drawn gun in the room, but because of the authoritative command of his voice.

"Now, let's get rid of the guns," ordered Luke.

Sheriff Cole noticed that both guns were pointed at him this whole time and cautioned his deputies to do exactly as told and do nothing foolish.

"One at a time, two fingers only, lay it on the table," ordered Luke. "Now, you, same procedure."

Luke then ordered the Sheriff to do the same. Luke laid one of his pistols on the table and frisked the two deputies and the sheriff one at a time. Still pointing the Colt at the Sheriff, he took the cell key from the customary hook on the wall and placed the two deputies in a cell and locked the cell door, then returned to the office with the Sheriff. He instructed the Sheriff to sit. Luke sat across the desk so he could look straight into Cole's eyes.

The Sheriff started to speak, and Luke interrupted, "I'm doing all the talking. You just have to listen. You are not going to like what I'm going to say and what I'm going to do. Your problem is that Quick Tender is innocent of murder."

"Says who?" Sheriff Cole blurted out.

Luke smashed the butt of the Colt in his right hand into Cole's mouth and nose that sent teeth and blood flying.

"We are running out of time. If you speak again without my permission, get mad, act defensively, or attack me, I will kill you on the spot. I want you to pay close attention. I will not repeat myself. You will do as I tell you to do, and when I tell you to do it, or I will kill you," reinforced Luke. "I have proof that Quick Tender was not on the prod for the Cole brothers. I have evidence that the Cole brothers were not deputies at the time they were killed. I have evidence that Quick Tender was twenty feet in front of and facing the Cole brothers when they were shot. I have proof that no gang broke Quick Tender out of jail."

Luke continued, "Now, more of your problem. If Quick Tender gets killed over your lies and reward money, I will personally chase you down and kill or hang you. I could go ahead and charge you with obstruction of justice, and see that you spend several years in prison."

Luke moved to face the Sheriff, "Now let me tell you my problem and how I'm going to solve it. I don't have time to get Quick a fair trial. I had rather do that so it would expose you to the whole world. He is innocent and would be set free, but there is no time. You had better hope one of your bounty hunters does not find him before you can get this fixed."

"I can't stand a low-down, crooked, low-life, lying scumbag like you. I started to just kill you just to rid the world of trash like you. I might let you live, but I'm taking your badge." Luke reached out and removed it.

"Now, for letting you live, you are going to do several things for me. You are going to send this telegraph to every newspaper and lawman that you sent the original fictitious story to. It says that it has been discovered that Quick Tender did act in self-defense in the killing of Melvin and Christy Cole. It says there was a misunderstanding about his release from jail, and that all charges and reward money has been withdrawn," instructed Luke. "It will also state that you have resigned from your position as sheriff, and you will never run for a public office again. Now, do you have any questions?"

"What if I don't sign?" inquired Cole.

"Sign it now," Luke said, as he tightened his hand around the grips of both guns. Brandon Cole knew he was not messing with a tenderfoot and was reaching for the pencil as soon as the three words had left the ranger's mouth.

Brandon signed the telegram, thinking he would have a better situation down the road. He had never had anyone talk to him the way this Texas Ranger Luke Shaw had, and he would not take it sitting down. He would get Luke Shaw and Quick Tender.

Luke directed Brandon Cole back to the cell and told him to tell his deputies he was no longer sheriff and to surrender their badges to him.

"Tell them yourself," he was saying when his body hit the ground as the result of Luke's swift blow to his head. Slapping Cole back to consciousness, he repeated his demand.

"Do as I say." Luke pulled back his hand for another slap when Brandon said, "I'm no longer Sheriff. Surrender your badges."

Luke took their badges and left the two men in the cell.

Luke took Brandon to the telegraph office. Just before arriving, Luke let out a prearranged whistle that signaled Ross to slip out the back door with Rainey.

Ross advised Rainey that Brandon Cole was no longer sheriff, and it might be wise for him to get out of the county. He pointed out that Brandon would know he signed a confession about lying that Quick Tender was on the prod for Melvin and Christy.

Luke entered the telegraph office and repaired the telegraph line. "Cole, tell Sam you are no longer the Sheriff, and you want to send this telegraph that you signed. Sam, you have the names."

Brandon responded immediately. "I am no longer the sheriff, and I want to send this telegram."

"Sam, after you send Brandon's telegraphs, send mine to the Texas Rangers. It is confessions, a list of evidence, and deposition of the case." Luke waited until all the telegraphs had been sent. He then returned with Brandon Cole to the Sheriff 's office.

Sam closed the telegraph office and ran all over town, telling everyone what had happened. People stayed off the streets but participated by looking out from behind curtains and joining close neighbors to gossip. With the knowledge that Brandon Cole would be loose made them want to stay out of sight until it was determined what he would do.

Luke placed Brandon in a cell, then opened the cell door that held Brandon's ex-deputies. "Boys, I'm going to give you a choice. I'm going to give you back your guns. You can ride out of the county peaceably and never again be associated with Brandon Cole, or we can have a shoot-out right now and settle the situation. Which will it be?"

"We will ride out." Both were very eager to leave.

"Remember this, if I ever hear of any association you have with Brandon Cole, I will hunt you down and kill you. What are your names?"

"Lance Long and Monty Crisp," they responded.

Luke stood at the door and saw the last dust settle from their horses racing out of town. He then turned his attention toward Brandon Cole. Luke brought Brandon to the front office and let him gather his personal belongings.

"Cole, you know how much I detest you and how much I want to kill you. I'm sure you feel the same about me. I'm going to give you back your guns and give you the opportunity. I'll let you put on your gun belt, then we will move out front, and I'll let you start the ball."

"No! I'm not going to put on my gun. I just want to ride out," said Brandon.

"Okay. But remember, if I ever catch you on my or Quick Tender's trail or offering money for our deaths, I will chase you until hell freezes over and kill you," threatened Luke. "Now, get your sorry ass out of my sight."

Luke Shaw sat down in the sheriff's chair with a smile on his face. He was pleased with the things that had happened this day and looked forward to hearing the feedback regarding how Brandon Cole and the two deputies reacted to being taken down. He was sure there would be some.

In a little less than an hour, there was a knock on the back door. Luke went to answer the knock he had anticipated. Letting Ross in, with a big smile, Luke asked, "Is it as I expected?"

"Yes. Rainey left as fast as his horse would let him, heading south. I hid in the loft of the stable," replied Ross. "Cole came in, saddled his horse, and waited for his two deputies. He dispatched them to find two of his cousins, Ray and Pike Cole." Ross continued,

"Lance Long and Monty Crisp will return as soon as they find Ray and Pike Cole. They figure you will check on your horse before dark. The Cole's plan to hide out in the barn and bushwhack you when you come in to check on your horse. Ray will take a position in the back of the barn. Pike Cole will be in the alley, catty-corner across the street, guarding the front. Lance and Monty will be backups, making sure you are killed," continued Ross.

"Luke, let me get inside the barn now and wait for Lance Long and Monty Crisp to return," planned Ross. "I can quickly disarm, gag, and tie them up. They don't know me, and I will be saddling my horse and complaining about the hostler not being around. I promise not to mess it up."

As Ross had been talking, he had removed Luke's two Colts. "It would be as easy as it was to remove your two guns without you knowing it."

Luke was embarrassed but shot back. "I've heard about sidewinders like you."

"Not like me. I'm an honest sidewinder," said Ross.

With sly grins on each of their faces, Luke conceded with, "You will do."

"Okay! Ross, before dark, I will walk to the barn, wait a few seconds, and fire a shot," planned Luke. "Then you take a position to take care of Ray Cole at the back door, and I will take care of Pike Cole at the front door. Ross, I want Brandon Cole for myself."

"Luke, I understand, but he needs killing," urged Ross.

"Ross, I don't plan to have a tea party with him," said Luke. "Did he say where he would be?"

"He said for them to take care of you," explained Ross, "and that he would be around to reclaim his sheriff position."

The stable was quiet when Ross entered. The hostler's office was open. It took only a few seconds for Ross to find the snakebite potion most hostlers kept to fight off the boredom of long hours. He splashed a liberal amount on his shirt and rinsed his mouth with a small portion, then disheveled his clothes. Ross put the bridle on his horse and led him out of the stall. He placed his saddle blanket unevenly across the horse's back and set the saddle on the ground at his side and waited.

About an hour before sunset, Lance and Monty returned. "Hey, hostler, where the hell you been? I need help saddling my horse," Ross said in a slurred voice.

"Mister, neither of us is the hostler, but if you will shut up, we will saddle your horse and get you out of here," offered Lance.

Lance moved forward, and as he approached, Ross maneuvered his horse between Lance and Monty. Ross stumbled around the horse and fell on top of his saddle. As Lance bent over to pick him up, Ross hit him in the solar plexus, knocking all the wind out of him, then hit him behind the neck, driving him to the ground unconscious.

"Help us over here. Your friend fell, and the horse stepped on him."

As Monty ran around in front of the horse, he ran into Ross's fist with the point of his chin. Ross tied both securely. He then stuffed and tied their bandanas in their mouths and pulled them into a stall. Ross put his horse back in his stall and waited for Luke.

As planned, just before dark, Luke came into the barn, took a look around, and fired his gun. A few seconds later, Ray Cole ran in the back door while Pike Cole ran in the front, each with their weapon ready to fire.

Ross and Luke stood in the middle of the stable, back to back facing them. Both had the advantage of the light.

As Ray Cole moved his gun toward Ross, Ross pulled his gun and fired at his favored target, which Paul had recommended. Ray did not raise up and dance on his tiptoes, as some do when shot. His head went back and he seemed to instantly crumple to the floor, dead. By this time, Pike Cole was dying from Luke's bullet to the heart. Luke and Ross went into the nearest empty stall and waited for Brandon Cole, with Luke reminding Ross that Brandon Cole was his. Brandon Cole never showed.

After waiting two hours, Luke and Ross pulled Lance and Monty out of their stall and took them back to jail.

After reminding them of his promise to kill them if they ever associated with Brandon Cole, Lance and Monty talked over each other, telling everything they knew. They revealed that Brandon Cole had lost all members of his posse, but Tommy Cole, Finley Cole, and Cliff Cole, all cousins of Melvin and Christy. They told Luke that Quick had been in Goldthwaite and now might be in San Angelo. Before today, Brandon and the three were getting ready to get back on Quick Tender's trail and stay on it until they, or the bounty hunters, killed him. Quick had ruined Brandon's life, and he was going to make sure he was killed.

Luke contacted the county commissioners and gave them a copy of Brandon Cole's resignation and a copy of the telegram that was sent to the newspapers and law officers. He asked that they appoint a new sheriff and told them of the two dead men in the stable and of his prisoners in jail. He told them he was filing charges against them for the attempted murder of Texas Ranger Ross Boudreaux and that he would be back for the trial.

Luke surmised that Brandon knew now of his failure to have him killed and was on his way to San Angelo.

Ross filled Luke in on the crew. He told about Paul Chambers being an expert tracker and being on Quick's trail from the graveyard. He told of Rafiel Fazio's and Boris Crewcheck's expertise and that they were with Paul. He then told of Jo Ling. He told all about his business talents but left out his martial arts talent. Jo Ling showed up at the sheriff's office just as Ross had finished. His small frame and perfect English, with no accent, gave no clue as to his powers.

A plan was needed for the fastest way to get to San Angelo. Ross could pull rabbits out of a hat, and Jo Ling could do the same with horses and carriages. Before noon the next day, Jo Ling showed up with a new carriage and four Missouri mules. Two were pulling, and two were following attached to the carriage with a double-tree rigging.

Missouri mules were famous for their sure-footedness and stamina. The rig was loaded down with supplies. The carriage had a spring on each axle and a springboard seat. Two could ride on the seat with plenty of room to spare. Jo Ling was an expert carriage handler.

Ross and Luke switched out scouting duties, and the mules were changed out as needed. They planned to travel from daylight till dark.

Most everything went well from the get-go. Luke had to use his Texas Ranger badge to persuade the ferry captain to get them across the Brazos River at Washington on the Brazos. He explained only once that he would take them across even though he had closed the ferry for the day.

Supplies were bought along the way as needed, and good time was being made. Luke wired Captain Smithhart their intentions. He wired back and told of a letter he had just received from Quick Tender. He congratulated Luke on the work he had done and stated that the letter, though not needed, would be additional proof of Quick Tender's innocence.

Information was sought on road conditions, Indians, bounty hunters, and Quick Tender. One piece of information that was picked up in Lampasas was that a bounty hunter by the name of Ryan Riemens was on the trail of Quick Tender in San Angelo. This prompted Luke to send a wire to Sheriff Sterling, seeking information on Ryan Riemens. The trio pulled out before any message was received.

CHAPTER 18:
QUICK TENDER'S RECOVERY

Quick slipped in and out of consciousness with fever and chills. His conscious hours were thinking about the things he wanted to tell the girl, which was everything. He had lost all reference of time, hours, days, and even weeks. His wounds from the large arrow were looking much better, and the chills and fever ceased. He began getting around without the crutch and was getting a full night's sleep. Quick planned to remove the stitches the next morning. He then was going to get on the girl's trail.

Quick had so much to tell the girl. He wanted to tell her everything before she heard rumors from others. The realization that he could not tell her anything until the Cut and Shoot incident was cleared up burdened him greatly. Quick checked his weapons and went to sleep.

Early the next morning, Quick built a small fire and heated his pick knife. When it was white-hot, he placed a stick in his mouth and bit down. He started burning the top of each stitch. Then using his thin-bladed knife, he pulled the thread out of the skin. Some was attached to the flesh and bled. These were cauterized with the hot pick to stop the bleeding. He then peeled the cambium layer off a large mesquite limb and placed it over the wound and tied it with strips from the boiled shirt.

Echo moved toward Quick with pointed ears toward the river. As Quick reached for his weapons, he heard a soft murmur. He moved to the edge of the plateau and, to his delight, saw his three Indian friends from the trading post. He spoke to them softly so as not to startle them, then directed them to the trail leading to the hideout.

They were glad to see him alive. They had been scouting for him several days to see if he had survived. It had been two weeks since he had left the trading post. They had reached De Leon on the fourth day after leaving the post and had news that a Comanche had been captured by an army patrol. He told them all the Comanche were leaving the area. Seems as if they had sixteen warriors killed with one bullet shot between each of their eyes. No other wounds entered their bodies.

He said they were leaving because it was an evil sign and bad medicine. They said the shooting happened in the surrounding area and wanted to know if he had heard any shots being fired. Not wanting to take any credit for the shootings, which would bring more attention to him, he told them about being hit by an arrow but escaped and found the hideout. He had been delirious with fever and chills and knew nothing as to what had happened to the Indians.

The Tonkawa reported that he had mailed his letter while in De Leon. Quick thanked him and took comfort to know that when anything was put in the mail, it was handled with privacy and respect.

Much talk swirled around about specific raids and lost lives. Without being obvious, Quick centered his inquiry on killed white women in the immediate area. They knew of none because most had gone to De Leon for safety. This was good news to Quick, but the killing of the sixteen Indians with the shot between their eyes would point directly to his whereabouts. He used the target for his safety on the first five and beyond all else the girl's safety on the last eleven.

He knew he would pay the consequences but would do so gladly to save the girl.

Quick expressed his desire to leave the area since the Comanches were gone. He also expressed his thanks to his three friends and told them he would continue to De Leon.

This was the first time in his life he had feared for his safety. It was because of the girl. Everything he did from now on had to include the safety and well-being of the girl. He mentally went through the complication the girl was creating. He declared himself crazy for even thinking about the girl. He had two murder charges for killing two supposedly deputies and a $1,000 bounty on his head. He escaped from jail and killed two gamblers and sixteen Indians. All twenty with a bullet between their eyes. He knew not if she was married or would ever think of someone with all the baggage hanging around his neck.

"I will just forget about the girl and head south to the gulf, buy a boat, and sail to Mexico," thought Quick. Why had he even considered being in love with this girl? Was it because she offered to help him? Ah! Probably, it being the first girl he had looked at since his realization of having no family. There would be others. He would go west, then turn south over the Colorado, then head to the Gulf of Mexico while everyone would be looking for him around here.

Who was he kidding? He was going to have the girl and raise a family, his family. That was final. I had rather be dead than be without the girl.

He formed a new plan. "William Peaceman" was now soiled goods. He decided on "Ryan Riemens." After repetitively signing the name, it was now his. This was bitter for Quick but had to be done. He would look forward to using Quick Tender again, a name he cherished.

Quick had never been trained on how to be an outlaw, but he seemed to see the necessity in thinking like one. He was changing his mind about staying away from largely populated cities. In a small city, he would be a new face, and everyone would be questioning as to who he was. In a large city, he would be just another face, but large or small, regardless of his safety, he had to find the girl.

The major trail to San Angelo from Goldthwaite was on the south side of the Colorado River. The Concho River ran into the Colorado near San Angelo. He remembered Plum Creek, which emptied into the Concho River, a few miles northwest of San Angelo. He would take this route and cross over the Concho at this point and enter San Angelo from this northwest direction. All eyes looking for him would be focused on his arrival being from the south side of the Colorado.

After removing the gold coins from the waistband of the torn and cut trousers, he dug a hole and buried the trousers and the torn shirt. He then placed a large rock over them to prevent animals from digging them up. He wanted to remove any evidence that would tie him to this location. He slipped on his boots. He tied the slit boot with the leather pig ties. He was eager to get on the way but did bury all evidence on him being there and wiped out his trail when leaving the hideout.

Quick's leg felt much better, and the riding seemed to help. This could be that it was taking him closer to finding the girl. Quick was always looking back for dust or sign of pursuers. He wanted to race to San Angelo as fast as he could but realized how foolish it would be. He did not know where the Indians had gone but knew there could still be war parties in the area. He did know the effort to capture or kill him would be concentrated in the area by lawmen or bounty hunters. A surprise meeting with either could be deadly, and he had to be patient. Each day he would circle back to see if anyone was on his trail. On the third day after leaving the hideout, to his dismay, he encountered two shod horses on his trail. Instead of following the horses, he turned around and went back the way he came.

Quick did not like the idea of being hunted. He was much more comfortable being the hunter. He moved off the trail and tied Echo loosely in a cluster of mesquite. He slipped off his boots and put on his moccasins. After hiding all signs of leaving the trail, he started his hunt. Moving off his previous trail by fifty yards, he moved back up the trail toward his pursuers. In approximately one-half mile, he heard them coming. He saw a movement on the trail about two hundred yards away. He moved in toward the trail, keeping low with plenty mesquite between him and his pursuers.

When they were within fifty feet, he stepped out into the trail with his rifle raised to his hip and his left hand on the belly-gun. There was a sudden reaction from the riders starting to reach for their guns. Both realized that Quick had an advantage, and to draw iron now would mean death for one or both. The riders decided that it might be better for them to try to talk their way out of the tight situation they were in or at least spread out and gain some sort of advantage. They had drawn their hands away from their guns before any words were spoken.

Quick told them to unbuckle their gun belts one at a time, and that if either of them caused any trouble, he would kill them both. He told them that if they were who he thought they were, they would be worth as much dead as alive.

There was hesitation from both riders. They tried to explain that they were not who Quick was hunting. Quick raised his rifle and pulled the Colt from his waistband and pointed at them, "First things first."

Quick pointed his rifle at the one on the right and said, "Unbuckle." The rider dropped it on the ground. Quick then looked to the second rider, "Now, you." He, too, dropped his rig to the ground. "Now you on the right take your rifle out of the scabbard and throw it off the trail," Quick instructed, "easy like with one hand." Looking to the other rider, "Now you," Quick instructed.

Quick walked backward for ten steps with a gun pointed at each. "Now, walk your horse forward ten steps and dismount. Tie your horse, then sit down on the ground."

Both had wanted to resist, but the bounty hunter had the upper hand and seemed to be a tough professional even as young as he appeared to be. He didn't act young. Quick had the two sit in the trail facing the sun. Quick sat in the shade and laid his Henry to the side. Quick sized up both. He figured both to be around thirty years old. Both looked mean and dirty.

"Now, we will talk. I will ask the questions. First you," he said, pointing his Colt at the older of the two. "What's your handle?"

"Don't know if that's any of your business."

Quick responded, "Since I'm a bounty hunter, I'm putting my dog in this hunt and making it my business."

Quick stood up and jerked the man to his feet while putting away his Colt. The man made a sweeping blow with his right hand, which Quick ducked under and grabbed the man by his throat. The other man was scrambling toward the discarded weapons. He screamed out in terror and pain. Quick had thrown a dagger that went through his right hand that had been reaching for the weapons.

Quick released the throat of the other man as he crumpled to the ground for lack of blood to the brain. He retrieved his dagger from the man's hand and pulled the man screaming and crying back to his sitting place. Quick took the bandana from the man's neck and threw it down to him. Still sobbing, he wrapped it tightly around his hand.

Quick told the man to stop whining and that he had brought it on himself. The other was regaining consciousness.

"Now, what is your name?"

"Joe Pike!"

"Ray Till!" said the other.

"Do either of you have a price on your head?" "No! No!" said in unison.

"Where are you from?" Quick asked.

"San Saba," both said.

"What are you doing out here other than following me?"

Joe Pike, still softly sobbing, said, "We'll be honest with you, mister. We heard of a seventeen-year-old outlaw, by the name of Quick Tender, had a $1,000 price on his head. We figured out where he might be and set out to earn some fast money. We figured as young as he was, he couldn't be as smart as we are, and he would be an easy catch."

Quick said he had not heard of Quick Tender but was on the trail of two outlaws that fit their description and would be taking them in. Joe and Ray both started protesting, which stopped when Quick added, "Dead or alive."

Quick needed to be rid of Joe and Ray so he could get back to hunting his girl. He would make them a deal they could not turn down. He told them they did not have enough sense to be good bounty hunters. He told them he did not like competition, good or bad, and that they had already wasted too much of his time. He told them he was going to let them go, but if he ever caught them on his trail again, he would kill them on sight.

Quick loaded up their weapons on their horses and told them they could pick them up five miles up the trail. He told them they would get on their horses and ride back to San Saba.

He told them he was going to take a nap nearby the horses and will see which direction they go when they find the horses. "If it's not San Saba, I will kill you both."

Joe Pike had stopped most of the bleeding in his hand, but it was swollen twice the size of a normal hand. He would not be shooting with his right hand soon, if ever. Ray Till thanked Quick for sparing their lives.

Quick rode off on Joe Pike's horse, and when out of sight and sound, he circled back to pick up Echo. He then rode up his old trail and left Joe's and Ray's horses.

CHAPTER 19:
SAN ANGELO

Quick had to have a plan. Being a bounty hunter just popped into Quick's head. Most of the bounty hunters after him would be new faces most anywhere they went. This might be the perfect cover he needed in this rural West Texas area.

He decided to go to the sheriff in San Angelo and tell him in confidence that he was a bounty hunter, and was in pursuit of Quick Tender. The sheriff would do the rest. He would tell one or two people, in confidence, who he was and who he was after, and by nightfall, everyone in town would know Ryan Riemens was a bounty hunter.

After crossing the north fork of the Concho River at Plum Creek, Quick found a wagon road that headed toward San Angelo. He took off his worn-out and slit boots and buried them. He repositioned his weapons taken from the boot and put on his moccasins. He then broke down his Henry and rolled it in his bedroll.

Quick followed the road south until the road forked. The most traveled road crossed back over the Concho. Quick stayed on the west side and entered what was considered Across the River by many of San Angelo's upper class. Across the River had several saloons and opium dens with gamblers and prostitutes. Along with that came fights, stabbings, and killings. This was not much different from some of the areas around most seaports that Quick had seen growing up.

He found the Mexican boot maker that lived there. Measurements were taken and promised the next day. It was not uncommon to see moccasins worn around town, but boots were a necessity for the trail.

There were several well-used low-water crossings on the Concho but only one bridge. The wooden bridge was seldom used unless rains made the river swell to unusual heights. Horses were frightened by the loud noise made while crossing the bridge. Quick used the bridge to bring as much attention as possible to the fact he was entering town from the west.

The sign on the building read the Sheriff's Office. The sign on the sheriff's desk read Sheriff Wesley Sterling. Quick asked the man behind the desk if he was Sheriff Sterling. An affirmative answer was given. Quickly and calmly, he introduced himself as Ryan Riemens. He told the sheriff that he wanted to come in to introduce himself because he was after a wanted fugitive and had lost his trail just outside of town. Quick wanted the Sheriff to know he was going to spend a few days in San Angelo. He also explained that he would be asking questions around town and wanted the sheriff to know in advance what was going on.

Sheriff Sterling asked if he was a bounty hunter. Quick responded that he did bring people accused of a crime in for a fair trial and give them a chance to tell their side of the story to a judge and jury. He pointed out that it could not happen if the accused did not survive their freedom.

The sheriff asked who he was after.

"I don't like to tell anyone who I'm after, but I do tell law officers and ask that they tell no one because it could get me killed."

"Oh! I would never tell anyone," promised Sheriff Sterling.

"Okay. It is a young man, seventeen years of age shot two men with one shot each between the eyes killing them, he said in self-defense. The two men had killed his father."

The sheriff jumped out of his seat and blurted out, "Quick Tender."

"Do you know him?" Quick asked.

"I don't know him, but I know of him," said the sheriff.

"Do you mind telling me what you've heard about him, Sheriff?" Quick asked.

"Sure, I'll tell you. The two men Tender killed were deputy sheriffs. They were supposed to be as tough as a wild boar hog. The sheriff said Tender bushwhacked them. He rode into town and told the hostler he was looking for them to kill them. The sheriff did say the deputies had killed Tender's father but killed him in self-defense. Tender was put in jail and charged with murder. The sheriff stated Tender's gang broke him out of jail. There was a dispute between what the sheriff said happened and what the townspeople say. They say Tender came out of the sheriff's office and announced that he had been cleared and calmly rode out of town."

Sheriff Sterling said Sheriff Cole did not mention that the Cole brothers had been shot between the eyes. Two men were killed in self-defense in Salado. They, too, had a single shot between their eyes. That news carried with it the information that the Cole brothers were killed with a shot between their eyes also. Sheriff Sterling said the Cole brothers might have been bushwhacked, but they had to be looking straight at Tender when he fired.

"In Salado, the shooter was described as a young tenderfoot kid who said he just got lucky with the two shots he made in the self-defense killings. He used the handle William Peaceman. If he was William Peaceman, he used the same target as Quick Tender, and Quick Tender is getting the credit for the self-defense killings."

"Mr. Riemens, you need to be careful on how you handle Quick Tender. Now, word is out that the sixteen Comanches that were killed near Goldthwaite had a single bullet between their eyes was also the work of Quick Tender. Many around here feel that he did a great service to the area."

Sterling also warned Quick of a Comanche hunting party in the area that killed a rancher and his family northeast of Plum Creek.

Quick asked if any raids were occurring now. Sterling told him most of the settlers and ranchers were now moving their families into town and letting the Comanche take what they wanted and hoping they would not be burned out.

Quick told Sterling he had other trails he was going to follow around San Angelo but figured Tender might have left the area. He pointed out to the sheriff that Tender spoke fluent Spanish and thought he was going to try to escape to Mexico.

"I want to remind you again, Mr. Riemens, you need to be careful because there seems to be more to the kid than most seventeen-year-olds even dream of. Being deadly accurate with a gun is one of them."

Quick assured the sheriff he would be, and that this was not his first rodeo. Quick thanked Sheriff Sterling for sharing the information on Quick Tender and asked again that he tell no one he was after Quick Tender because he wanted to bring him in alive.

After leaving the sheriff's office, Quick slowly rode down the main street, looking straight ahead but seeing every building, every roof, every door, every sign, and every alley. He saw every person on the street but did not see the girl or her companion.

When he reached the Concho, he made a mental note. The north fork of the Concho angled to the south and was joined by the Middle Concho River, then emptied into the Colorado. He returned down a back street to the livery stable he had seen on his ride to the Concho. A better-class saloon, café, and hotel were near.

After rousting out the hostler and paying for Echo's care, Quick took his saddlebags and bedroll and went across the street to the hotel. Quick was sleepy and hungry but could not wait to begin the search for his future wife and mother of his many children to come. Ryan Riemens checked in and took a room on the second floor.

The room was at the top of the staircase, and the door could be seen from the lobby. When leaving, he left his saddlebags and bedroll under his bed. There was no easy entry from the only window. After checking all his weapons, he stuffed the lock with a bar of soap and jammed the key halfway in and broke it off in the lock. After wiping all the soap residue from the lock, Quick went down the stairs, out the door, and into the cafe. There were six customers, all men. His heart sank.

How stupid am I? Of course, she would not be in the first place I look. But I know she's close. Wait a minute! I don't have a plan. What would I have done if she had been present?

"Coffee?" the waitress asked.

"Yes, please," replied Quick.

Quick was suddenly not hungry. "That's all for now," said Quick.

What would I have done? Quick thought, I only know two things about women. I'll start there and add on as I learn more. One is, be hard to get. Two is to be protective of her, which I was not the first time I saw her. I could not bring myself to kill her companion but should have. Quick shook his head. He was so confused. He felt sure of himself, and his confidence had not suffered but knew this woman could be his Achilles' heel. He thought through his plan. He would lie low and hide from her until he could find out more about her situation.

When he did expose his existence, he would need time and space to tell his side of the story. He would tell her everything. Maybe everything except how rich he was. Quick smiled and ordered his meal.

Upon leaving the cafe, Quick noticed a young man leaving just in front of him. Quick followed him until he stopped and was looking in a display window. Quick tapped on his shoulder, extended his hand with a big smile on his face, and introduced himself as Ryan Riemens.

The young man turned. "Ben Russel here," he said.

Quick said he was new in town and had seen him in the cafe and thought he might be able to tell him where he might meet some good-looking, nice girls.

Ben said, "Not many in town, but there will be soon. There was an Indian raid this morning, killing a rancher and his family, and that it could be part of the Comanche tribe that was driven out of Goldthwaite. Regardless of where they came from, the ranchers would be bringing in their families until this is over. There should be several lookers in that bunch."

"Maybe you could introduce me to some of them," Quick said. "And by the way, who drove the Comanche out of Goldthwaite?"

"A young outlaw by the name of Quick Tender. Shot sixteen of them between the eyes. If the Comanche stay around here, the town-hopping Quick Tender will show up here."

"Nice meeting you, Ben. If you see any of those cute girls, tell them Ryan Riemens is on the prowl."

Returning to the hotel, Quick went upstairs to his room. Turning around from any spying eyes, he reached behind his neck and took out his pick. He fished out the broken key and then turned the tumblers with the pick faster than he could have unlocked the door with the key. He eased into the room and placed the one chair in the room under the doorknob. He checked his saddlebags and bedroll, making sure nothing had been disturbed. He moved the bed to the other side of the room, then placed his weapons in easy reach of the bed.

After a needed night of sleep, Quick awoke with the rumble of a busy little city. More so than when he went to sleep. Looking in the small framed mirror nailed into the wall, Quick did not recognize himself. Looking back at him was a twenty or twenty-one-year-old with a dark complexion. He had a scraggly black beard and piercing blue eyes. So much for the tenderfoot image. He was a tough, confident bounty hunter and was looking for Quick Tender.

Even though he needed a shave, he opted to leave the face as is and just bathe in the basin and change into clean clothes. When dressing, Quick realized the clothes had shrunk, or he had grown a lot in the past few months. He checked his weapons and replaced them on his body. He left the Henry in the bedroll. Pulling his hat lower toward his eyes, Quick stood aside from the door and slightly opened it. He saw a lot of motion in the lobby. After a small hesitation and seeing no danger, Quick eased into the hall and inserted the broken key and started down the stairs. He saw nine men milling around the lobby. Most of them stared at him, then eased out the door. Good! The word was out. They had come to see what the bounty hunter that was looking for Quick Tender looked like.

At the sidewalk, Quick waited in the shade until his eyes adjusted to the bright morning sun. The street was packed with groups of people and numerous parked buggies. Others were looking for a place to park. Quick looked at every face. He did not want to miss the two he was now hunting. Quick eased his way to the cafe. It was packed but found a single table next to the kitchen and back door. This would be perfect, he thought. Without staring, he observed each table and the occupants. He saw several that had stared at him as he walked in. They were now discussing if he was the bounty hunter.

Quick ordered coffee, bacon, and eggs. Quick was served the coffee and was told there would be a wait on the rest. Quick seemed to be concentrating on the coffee but was listening in on all conversations he could hear. With interest, he strained to hear about the Comanche being driven out of Goldthwaite by the outlaw Quick Tender.

Other conversations were about ranchers that had not shown up with their families. One woman expressed her worries about Kathy Gale. To her knowledge, she was still at her ranch. Her Uncle was in a card game here in town and was not going to risk going after her. They talked highly of her ability to take care of herself but admitted she would not have a chance if caught in a raid. There was mention of a ranch being raided and burned near Sterling City, but it was confirmed that it was not Kathy Gale's. She also talked about how terrible she thought it was that her father had appointed his worthless brother guardian over Kathy Gale.

When Kathy Gale's name was mentioned, in his heart, he felt she was the one. Could it be? Just in case, he had to act now. Just in case!

When his meal was served, he asked to pay for it now and would wolf it down, so someone else could have his seat. He had to be careful. He had to find this card game and Kathy Gale's uncle. Just in case!

Quick was relevantly certain he would not be Across the River. He thought of only one place he should be. When he reached the front swinging door to the saloon and gambling hall, he stood aside and closed his eyes for a few seconds. He then stepped through the door and moved to his left three paces and stopped. By then, he had made a complete survey of the entire room. He had located the bar with the door behind it, for future reference, and the three poker tables. Quick moved to the far end of the bar, ordered a beer, and turned facing the room in search of the face he wanted to see. This proved to be unnecessary. At that moment, Sheriff Sterling burst into the room and called out Calvin Chambers.

"Calvin! What are you going to do about getting Kathy Gale and bringing her here?"

"Nothing," Chambers replied. "She's a grown woman and can take care of herself."

"Calvin, she's a sixteen-year-old girl who we all know can ride and shoot as well as any man, but she can't handle an Indian raid."

It was everything Quick could do to prevent from putting Calvin in his sight again, but this time pull the trigger.

Sheriff Sterling wheeled and went for the door. Quick was right behind him.

Hailing the sheriff, Quick asked if he had a plan to rescue the young lady and the other ranchers that had not shown up.

"I've notified the Texas Rangers. The closest company is in Colorado City. Twenty rangers should be on their way headed by Captain Bryan Marshall."

Many thoughts rushed through Quick's mind. The main thing was for him to remain calm. He needed time to figure out his approach toward the rangers. Quick knew of the captain. It was said that he was a hard-drinking ex-rebel that put up with no-nonsense.

But first things first, and that was rescuing the girl. The love of his life.

Quick told Sheriff Sterling he had planned to drift up toward Sterling City. His thinking was that in case Quick made it close to San Angelo, he might have decided to skirt the town and go up the Concho to the smaller town of Sterling City.

The sheriff suggested that he might ought to sit tight until the raids stopped.

Quick told the sheriff that he was not going to stop his pursuit of Quick Tender for any reason. He would gladly look in on the girl while in the area if he had the directions to Calvin's ranch.

"It's not Calvin's ranch. It belongs to Kathy Gale. Her father, Ben Chambers, died when Kathy Gale had just turned fourteen years old. Ben left the ranch to Kathy Gale and appointed Calvin as her guardian until she turned eighteen or married. Calvin has run off any suitor that showed any interest in her. The problem there was that all the boys showed an interest, and Calvin keeps her isolated at the ranch," said Sheriff Sterling.

Sheriff Sterling went on and told Quick that the ranch once belonged to his uncle, Captain Sterling. The captain was a buffalo hunter and ranched the Concho Valley. He had singlehandedly ran the Comanche from the Valley by killing Indians from five hundred to eight hundred yards with his Sharps buffalo gun. When all the buffalo were gone from the area, he sold the ranch to Kathy Gale's father, Ben Chambers, and moved to Colorado.

"Where's the ranch?" Quick asked.

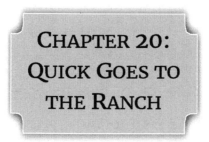

CHAPTER 20:
QUICK GOES TO
THE RANCH

The ranch is on the west side of the Concho, forty-five miles out, and one mile from the Concho. It's a hard day's ride if you head straight for it and have a good horse."

"Thanks, Sheriff, if I run into Quick Tender, I might ask him to help us."

"That would be great if he would," he replied.

Quick rushed to the hotel and paid for one-month rent in advance. He grabbed his saddlebags and bedroll and rushed to get Echo. Echo was rested, well-fed, and ready to get on the road. Quick rode west and opted to cross the river at one of the many low-river crossings and bypass the wooden bridge. He headed to the bootmaker and retrieved his new boots. He replaced the knife and gun that went in the sewn-in scabbards for each, then headed further west. Upon leaving sight of town, Quick pulled aside and waited ten minutes to see if he had any followers. Seeing none, he swung north for a mile. He then stopped and walked back, covering all signs.

Quick returned to Echo and retrieved the Henry from the bedroll. Mounting Echo, Quick moved out at a steady and cautious pace. He dared not go at a faster pace, knowing that any moment,

Echo might be called on for a fast and lengthy race, avoiding Comanche warriors.

The main road to Sterling City was on the east side of the Concho, but Quick thought the west side trails would be safer. The terrain had become rougher with numerous arroyos and plateaus with decreasing vegetation. Some of the plateaus were long and winding, for several miles, with deeper arroyos to handle the water runoff. Quick was questioning his decision of going up the west side of the Concho instead of the east. Could he reach the ranch by tomorrow?

It was getting late, and Quick had put in a hard day's ride. He had only stopped once, and that was to water Echo. It was about that time again. Seeing a game trail leading off to the northeast, Quick took it and found the Concho in less than a mile. Quick let Echo drink his fill and moved out on a much dimmer game trail heading northwest. He found a suitable place to camp near a plateau and stopped just before dark.

Quick would not risk building a fire. He would eat jerky and let Echo graze and stand guard. Quick went to sleep thinking of Kathy Gale and woke up doing the same. Awake before daylight, Quick resisted climbing to the top of the plateau and looking around. If anyone were around, it was dark enough to make it to the top without being seen. Going down was a different story. He could not risk having to sit tight until nightfall to get off the plateau. He had to get to the ranch.

He moved out, skirting the plateau. He stopped to look back and saw an interesting formation on the east face of the plateau. It could not be seen until you were past it. He wanted to climb up for a better look, but for the sake of time, he turned and rode back to make sure the small plateau could not be seen from a southern direction. After confirming this, he decided he would keep this in mind for future reference. He headed north.

It was a long and grueling day. Echo needed water. Moving back to the northeast, he again hit the Concho. After Echo had his fill, Quick removed his saddle and let him have a good roll. Both were hungry and tired, but Quick was determined to reach the ranch before dark. It was hard for Quick to judge distance, having to go around plateaus and finding a way out of the many arroyos. He remembered studying the area on maps with his grandfather. His guess was he was five to ten miles from the ranch. Resaddling Echo, they moved out.

Drifting northwest and about to head north, Echo stopped with his ears darting in all directions. Quick raised the Henry and drew the Colt from his waistband. From the south was a swirl of dust. This was no dust devil. Quick swung Echo due north at a dead run. Directly in front of Echo, a Comanche had jumped in his path with a bow drawn ready to release an arrow. Echo knocked him several yards backward, rendering the arrow harmless and the Indian unconscious. In passing the Indian, Quick reached down and snatched the Indian off the ground and over the saddle in front of him. The Indian only had the wind knocked from him and started to stir. Quick reached down and grabbed him around the neck, cutting off the blood supply to his brain.

Echo had been running, all out, for over a mile and started slowing down. Looking behind him, nine Indians were in sight and gaining.

Looking ahead was a clearing. The mesquite had been cleared, and a ranch house and outbuildings could be seen approximately eight hundred yards ahead. Echo realized the urgency as much as Quick and responded with a new burst of speed. The ranch house was getting closer. Quick fired three shots in the air to get the attention of anyone in the house. He saw movement and saw the door swing open. As Echo cleared the low wooden fence enclosing the yard, Quick saw the flowers that Echo was landing in at that time. He lowered his head to clear the door as Echo slowed to enter. The door closed as the thuds of arrows striking the door sent a chill down Quick's spine.

Echo settled down, and Quick was staring down the barrel of a gun held by a mad woman.

"You crazy, idiot! Bringing a war party to my home, tearing up my flower beds, and what is that lying over your saddle?"

With a slight smile on his face, he softly spoke. "I can explain, ma'am," Quick said as he reloaded his Henry. "First, let me change the direction of those Indians. You keep an eye on the Indian here. Shoot him if you have to, but I would like him kept alive."

Quick turned to one of the gun portholes in the wall and fired three shots, killing three of the Indians with one shot each between the eyes. Then he turned and reloaded his Henry. He could have killed more, but he just wanted to get their attention.

He turned and stammered. He was looking in the eyes of his future wife and the mother of his future children. He was certain of it. He took a deep breath, gathered his senses, and said, "That will take care of them for a while."

Kathy Gale was standing with her mouth open, unable to utter a word. Who was this man? Why in the hell is he smiling? Why would he want to keep this Indian alive? Why did he not kill more of the Indians?

"Do you have any hands around close?" Quick asked.

"No! I have four hands. Two are in the line shack on the north end of the ranch, and the other two are on the west side. All four are at least five miles away. We didn't expect any trouble and had more work to do out on the range than here," Kathy Gale replied.

"I've got to talk to this Indian. Do you sign, speak Comanche, or Spanish?"

"No!" said Kathy Gale.

This was the answer Quick desired. "Ma'am, keep an eye on the Indians outside while I talk to this one."

Quick took his canteen and wet down his bandana. After a few minutes, the Indian regained consciousness. He attempted to rise until Quick gripped the muscle going down from the Indian's neck to his shoulder. The Indian writhed down in pain. Quick started signing, speaking Spanish, Cherokee, Tonkawa, and the few Comanche words he was sure of, then settled on mostly Spanish and signing. He told the Indian he was the medicine man for the white man, and that he had taken Captain Sterling's place when he left the area. "I am the medicine man that killed sixteen of your brothers near Goldthwaite on the Colorado with a single shot between their eyes. Three of your brothers lie dead out front with a single shot between the eyes. You are to go and retrieve your dead brothers and return them to your tribe. Tell them they are to leave and never return to this part of the country again. Tell them that I do not like to kill, but that I do have one bullet for each of them if they do not leave. Usted entiende?"

"Si!" the Indian replied.

Quick led the Indian to the door. Kathy Gale called out, "You fool, what are you doing?"

"I'm letting him go, ma'am," was Quick's reply.

"If you call me ma'am one more time, you are going to go out with him," Kathy Gale retorted.

Still holding the Indian tightly, Quick asked, "What do you want me to call you?"

"My name is Kathy Gale Chambers. You are to call me Miss Chambers. Who are you?"

"I'm Ryan Riemens, ma-uh, Miss Chambers," Quick responded.

"What are you doing here?" Kathy Gale asked.

"I rode out of San Angelo yesterday with intentions of looking for someone of interest to me. I told Sheriff Sterling I would check on you and see if you were safe or needed help getting to safety," Quick explained.

"Safety from what?" she asked.

"There's been Comanche Indian raids in the area for the last three days with several burned-out ranches and killings. The Texas Rangers have called out twenty of their troops but will not be here for a couple of days," stated Quick.

"I have felt perfectly safe here for sixteen years until you rode into my life with a live Indian across your saddle and whooping Indians on your tail. Now you only kill three of nine, and you want to let this one leave. That does not make me feel secure from the Indians or you."

"I'll release him. I gave him information that will make his tribe want to leave the area." Opening the door, Quick pushed the Indian out.

"Oh, you think they would be afraid of the twenty rangers?" she asked.

"No! I had to release him for our safety. I'll try to explain later," stated Quick

"Who is the person of interest you mentioned?" questioned Kathy Gale.

"He is a man in deep trouble. I want to catch him and take him in, so he can clear his name, and then, of course, there is you," responded Quick.

"Why should I be of interest to you? I don't have a bounty on my head."

"Ma'am! Uh, miss, you are taking this all wrong. Let me explain."

"You've already told me you are hunting a man in deep trouble. Most men have a reason to hunt men in trouble. The reason being money. Those men are called bounty hunters. No explanation needed. Now you tell me you have an interest in me, and it's not a bounty. You are just like all the other cowboys that come around. Promising me love but are after my ranch. At least, they are not bounty hunters."

Still, with the constant smile on his face that was about to drive Kathy Gale crazy, he spoke, "Miss Chambers, we certainly got off on the wrong foot. I can't explain why I'm hunting a man in deep trouble, but it's not money. That's the truth. As for you, Ryan Riemens is not a cowboy, and he will never promise love and try to take your ranch. I don't want a ranch. I know very little about ranching and less about cows or women. So don't waste your time wondering what I'm after. I will tell you this. I am going to protect you from the Indians and what else comes along, whether you like it or not. I want you to look out the gun ports on the back wall, and make sure no Indians approach us from that direction, then be quiet and let me concentrate."

Reaching for his saddlebag, he retrieved his looking glass and rushed to a porthole. The released Indian had reached the three dead. Their three horses had been gathered by the six remaining Indians of the chase. They were signaled by the released Indian for them to come to him. There was commotion and excitement around the bodies. The bodies were gathered and placed over two of the horses. The released Indian rode one.

Going back to the edge of the south clearing with the telescope, Quick saw that the Indians seemed to be having a heated powwow. A few minutes later, the released Indian and two others rode off with the bodies. Quick followed their sight for several miles by watching the dust cloud put up by their speedy exit. The other four dismounted on the edge of the mesquite and started a small fire.

This signaled bad news for Quick. He did not know where their main force was but was sure the three were going after a larger party while the four were left behind to keep them pinned down. The information he had given the released Indian might backfire on him. His capture or death could be the greatest coup of all the Comanche. It took Quick only a few minutes to come up with another plan.

The Comanche had not followed his demand that they clear out of the area. As bad as he disliked killing Indians, he had no alternative but to kill the four left behind. He had to put a bullet between each of their eyes. This had to be done before the other Indians returned. It would be dark soon, and he would leave on foot. He would leave Echo in the house to protect him from being stolen by the Indians.

"Miss Chambers, I've got to leave and take care of some important business," explained Quick.

"Oh! You stir everything up, and now you are running out? I guess I shouldn't expect anything else from a bounty hunter. But one thing, you're not leaving here without me!" exclaimed Kathy Gale.

"Look," Quick said. "I'm going on foot. I won't be gone but an hour or so, and I'm going to be in a hurry. When I'm through, I will return."

"I can walk as fast as any man, and I'm going," said Kathy Gale. "I can't let you go. It would be too dangerous, and I don't want you to see what I have to do," Quick said.

"What do you have to do?"

"I have to kill four Indians, and I have to kill them now."

"I've seen Indians killed, and I have killed some myself. I'm going! I'd rather die outside rather than here alone," Kathy Gale said.

"Do you have moccasins?"

"Yes!"

"Then put them on," grumbled Quick, "You must promise to do exactly what I tell you to do. If the four are still together, I will kill them all at once."

"You going to use a stick of dynamite?" she asked.

"No, but it may sound like it with all the shooting you will hear," Quick explained.

"I want to back you up," she said.

"No! It would be too dangerous. If the Indians have separated, I will hide you and stalk them until I find them. I will return to you when the killin's done. We need to make sure to get their horses then ride back to the ranch house."

"Will we try to go back toward San Angelo tonight?" Kathy Gale asked.

"No, it would be too dangerous," explained Quick. "Your ranch house will be easier to defend, if necessary. Three Indians rode off with the bodies of the three I killed. They were headed southwest. I'm sure they will return in the morning with a war party. They must find the four that I have to kill."

Quick took one last look through the telescope. He found where the horses were and gauged their location in relation to the Indians.

Quick and Kathy Gale would have to stay downwind of the horses and the Indians to not be located.

While getting on their moccasins, Quick laid out his plan. The two of them would go out the back door, ease over to the barn, and go due west until they reached the mesquite. Then they would go south about two hundred yards past where the Indians were now and come at them from the south. Most of the four Indians' attention would be to the north, watching the ranch house. Their horses would be in hand before Quick would move in for the kill.

Quick grabbed the Henry and extra shells. He checked all his weapons then asked to see Kathy Gale's. He looked over her weapon, also a Colt .45, and instructed her to keep it in her hand. He then handed her a single .45 bullet with instructions to put it in her pocket. Gently, he put his hand on her shoulder and looked in her eyes. "Do not be taken alive under any circumstance, Miss Chambers." He also told her he would give his life to save hers. She thought that that was a mighty strong statement coming from a bounty hunter. Who was this guy? How in the world could he be so sure of himself?

Just before leaving out the back door, he instructed Kathy Gale to stay low and about twenty yards behind him until they reached the mesquite. When they arrived at the bushes, he told her not to let him get out of her sight and for her to stop each time he did.

They had made good time, only slowing when coming to the end of the clearing. Quick took out his scope and located the four Indians. They were all around the small fire. The horses were still in the same place he had seen them earlier. This was good news for Quick.

Quick and Kathy Gale moved on past. When they got to the desired two hundred yards past the Indians, Quick stopped and again checked his weapons. He slung the Henry, barrel down, over his shoulder, and drew both his Colt .45s. He felt guilty doing this, but this was a life-or-death situation, especially with Kathy Gale's presence.

The four Indians were still by the fire with their horses to the southwest of them. He moved to the east to keep from startling the horses. Quick stopped, looked back, and found Kathy Gale. He eased back to her and placed his hand on her shoulder and whispered, "This will be over soon. Stay tight to the mesquite to your right, and I will come for you."

Kathy Gale reached out and touched Quick's shoulder and whispered, "Why don't we just shoot them from here?"

Quick shook his head "no" and turned away.

Kathy Gale's heart was pounding as he walked toward the Indians. She felt she had to back him regardless of what he had told her. She thought it was next to impossible for one man to kill four Indians without being killed or wounded himself. She wanted to do her part and would die if necessary. She could not understand why Ryan was so stubborn about killing them all at once.

Kathy Gale moved forward with gun in hand. She could see Ryan moving forward toward the fire. The four Indians sat with rifles in their laps. They were facing north.

Quick moved forward rapidly. Kathy Gale's first thought was that the fool was going to commit suicide. Before she could react to help, the four Indians were turning and rising to face Quick. With the first shots, the two Indians farther away were dead and falling to the ground. When the second two shots fired, the other two were joining them.

Quick calmly reloaded his Colts, knowing all four had one bullet between their eyes and were no longer a threat.

Kathy Gale, in total shock, could not believe what she had just seen and was frozen in position.

Before turning to face her, Quick spoke softly with a slight smile still on his face. "I thought I told you to stay put." He then turned. Seeing how shaken she was, he went to her and put his hands on her shoulders and whispered, "I didn't want you to see this. We will talk later. We have to go."

Gathering the four mustangs, Quick picked out the largest one and suggested he would mount him and get all the bucking out of him, if any. Kathy Gale was to hold the other three mustangs. After three stiff-legged bucks and three turns, the mustang settled down. Quick moved the mustang over close to Kathy Gale, reached down, and gently picked her up, placing her on the mustang's bareback behind him.

"Hang on tight," he instructed as she placed her hands around his waist. Quick took the lead ropes of the three other mustangs and moved out slowly.

He moved to the west side of the clearing and headed north to the barn. No further words were spoken, but Kathy Gale's thoughts were running wild. More wild things had happened to her in the last four hours than in a lifetime.

She was embarrassed for thinking of him as Ryan and not Mr. Riemens. Who was this guy? Who makes plans in a second and carry them out thus far? This bounty hunter who killed three Indians with three shots and could have killed the other six that chased him to the ranch. With the ability he had with a gun, he was not only a bounty hunter but must also be a gunfighter. Neither have good reputations, she thought.

Who was this guy that would release an Indian to give a message and would go out and kill four Indians at the same time because the direction in his message had not been followed? Why was he so sure and confident that he could kill four Indians with four shots that sounded like two? It was also mighty strange that none of the Indians moved, other than to the ground, once shot.

Also, how could he be so gentle with her after all the terrible things she had said to him in the last four hours and still have a slight smile on his face? Why does he seem vaguely familiar?

Quick felt certain no other Indians were in the vicinity. Even if they were, they would be heading toward the shots instead of the ranch house. This would give him plenty of time to prepare for an attack.

Reaching the ranch house, Quick dismounted and eased Kathy Gale to the ground. He tied the mustangs to the fence and cautiously moved toward the front door. Echo was glad to see them and nuzzled them both. Once inside, Quick told Kathy Gale his plan for the four mustangs.

Both were hungry, and Kathy Gale prepared food while Quick took Echo and the four other mustangs to the barn. Using a shielded match, Quick located the ladder to the loft where he pitched down hay. The water trough was full. He let the mustangs and Echo have their fill and then put the four Indian ponies in empty stalls. He let Echo roam about freely to be on alert.

Quick found the pile of fencepost Kathy Gale had mentioned when she heard the plan. He located the one he thought was the heaviest and dug it out of the pile. It was a corner post. He leaned it next to the barn door and left the barn door open for easy access.

After returning to the house, they ate in silence. After eating, Quick inspected all the portholes for possible dead spots. A lot of thought had been put into the layout of the house. The kitchen was in one corner. A hand-dug well with a hand pump was near. Kathy Gale said it produced an abundance of water. Kathy Gale's room was next to the east wall. It had a thick double shutter over the window.

Quick removed the bars and opened the shutters inwardly on all the windows. He needed access to the many sounds from the outside. He asked Kathy Gale to move her bedding to the wall near him so he would know where she was in the dark in case shooting started. He asked to check her weapon. Then he had her place it next to the wall close to her head, so she would know where it was in the dark.

Quick reassured her that he did not expect any attack until after daylight. He was going to sleep but would trust Echo to alert him of any danger. He encouraged her to sleep and get all the rest she could and reminded her he would be waking her up around midnight. Checking his weapons, he settled in and soon was sleeping soundly.

Kathy Gale could not sleep. She did not want to go to sleep. This guy was strange. Ryan looked like a cowboy but wasn't. He was much cleaner than any cowboy she had ever seen. He was a very striking person, especially with that slight smile that seemed to always be present. It had been hard for her to keep her eyes off him.

Why did he look familiar? She had never met a bounty hunter. He moved with such ease, regardless of the situation. He never exhibited a show of fear, just confidence. Does being a bounty hunter give you this confidence?

Ryan showed a reluctance to kill the Indians but showed no emotion when he did. Does this come from being a bounty hunter? She could not make up her mind if she liked him or not, but knowing how ruthless the Comanche were, she was glad he was with her now.

She was now only thinking of him as Ryan instead of Mr. Riemens. Did he care if she liked him or not? Does the slight smile mean he knows something that she doesn't? It seemed that it could be that he didn't care for her. He said in plain words that Ryan Riemens will never promise her love. But he was nice and had

143

treated her with nothing but respect. He must just be chivalrous. How in the world would a bounty hunter get that trait?

"I've got to know more about Ryan. Maybe he could change. I'm going to make him like me!" she proclaimed.

Quick slept sparingly, waiting on midnight. He would often awaken just to hear Kathy Gale breathe. He wanted to start planning his future with her. There were so many obstacles that had to be solved before he should even think about it. But think he did.

The first obstacle was the Indians. What if they returned with the whole tribe, which numbered over three hundred? What if the coup of capturing or killing him was such a temptation that the bravest of the brave could not resist? Would his bluff bring on his final demise? The cards were dealt.

Nothing he could do now would change the number of Indians that would show or the action they would take. He had to stick with his plan. The four dead Indians at the edge of the clearing could be a deciding factor, or it could be the Indian mustangs. Foremost in his mind would be to protect Kathy Gale while playing hard to get. A slight grin swept across his stern face.

Kathy Gale awoke with a gentle hand over her mouth, and Quick's whisper, "It's time."

Quick had closed all the windows and placed the bars back on the shutters except the one he would now exit.

"Please come back, Ryan," pled Kathy Gale while slightly shivering.

Quick squeezed her shoulder and left out the open window and headed to the barn.

"Wow! She called me Ryan," thought Quick.

Kathy Gale guarded the open window as planned.

Quick gathered the lead ropes on the Indian mustangs in one hand and mounted Echo, who was without his bridle or saddle. He would guide him with his knees. He checked his weapons and moved to the barn door. Here he reached out and grasped the heavy fence post, laid it over Echo's shoulders, and started out.

Looking skyward, he located his bearings and within ten minutes, located his desired location. Easing off Echo with the fence post, Quick tied the mustangs to the fence post, facing each other. Remounting, he rode back toward the house. Stopping, he let loose his prearranged signal of a far off lonesome nighthawk. Kathy Gale gave her an all-clear signal of a soft-spoken, "Echo."

Quick released Echo, knowing he would stay close and eased back in the open window. Kathy Gale could not resist reaching out and hugging him. Quick was grateful that it was pitch dark as that would cover his true feelings.

Gently placing his hands on her arms and holding her at a short distance, Quick whispered, "Miss Chambers, you just hugged someone you think is a bounty hunter."

"But you told me you were not," Kathy Gale silently retorted

"But you still think I am," Quick said with a sly smile.

"I don't know what to think. I'm so afraid," Kathy Gale whispered.

"I told you I would protect you to my death," he reassured.

"I'm afraid for you as I am for myself," she said.

"I'm very capable of taking good care of myself just as I am of you. Let's try to get a little more sleep and discuss this later," said Quick.

"I want to discuss it now!" she stated.

"There is nothing to discuss now! We must survive the impending attack. Lie down, try to get some sleep. Echo will alert us of any danger," asserted Quick.

Kathy Gale knew he was right. It was likely that they both would be killed, and she did not want the last hours of her life to be spent sleeping. She wanted them to be spent being held and loved even by a bounty hunter. She knew if she were not in this situation, she would not give Ryan a second look. It has to be this situation that has made her not able to keep her eyes off him and caused the desire to hug and hold him close to her.

A while later, Kathy Gale awoke. She found Ryan looking through his telescope.

"Good morning, sleepyhead! I've taken the liberty of inventorying your weapons," stated Quick. "I've looked through every porthole and have not seen any movement. I've placed your six Winchesters and two shotguns in the portholes ready to fire and shells on the floor beneath them. When attacked, don't worry about saving ammunition. Just keep firing, as long as you have someone to shoot. I don't think we will need the Sharps buffalo gun now, but it is loaded."

Quick continued, "Let's make sure we shoot from every gun port. Wouldn't want them to know there were only two of us. If you get overwhelmed, just call out, and I will shift positions with you. The portholes have no blind spots, and we have a good view of the barn. The mustangs are still in the clearing undisturbed."

"Let's fix something to eat. Might be too busy later on," suggested Quick.

"Let me do that," offered Kathy Gale.

"Thanks, Miss Chambers," offered Quick.

"Please, just call me Kathy Gale."

"I will if you will call me Quick—as the food is ready, and please call me Ryan," Quick promptly corrected.

"I will, Ryan. Where is Echo?"

"He is standing by peaceably in the barn."

Kathy Gale brought a plate of food to the window where Quick was seated.

"Thank you, Kathy Gale."

Kathy Gale reached out and grabbed the shutter to steady herself. Why would her knees go out from under her and make her nearly pass out just because he called her Kathy Gale?

"You alright, Kathy Gale?"

"Uh, sure, just stumped my toe."

The sun was coming up, and no Indians were in sight. Around ten o'clock, Echo came to the window, alerting Quick. His ears were perked up and pointed southwest. Quick gently pulled on his ears and hugged his neck and sent him back to the barn with a signal to stay.

Am I going crazy? Kathy Gale thought. *I'm about to be killed by Indians, and I'm wanting this bounty hunter to pull on my ears and hug me!*

Quick picked up the telescope and saw nothing but the mustangs in the middle of the clearing and the dead Indians at the edge of the mesquite. He raised the scope to see over the mesquite trees and saw a large cloud of dust rising from the southwest.

"I didn't expect this many," he said to Kathy Gale. "I'm sure some will leave when they see the four dead."

"Ryan, why would some leave when they see the four dead Indians?" she questioned.

"I can't explain now, but trust me, some will leave," stated Quick.

"I'm sure they have seen their dead brothers before. What's so special about those four?" Kathy Gale continued.

"Just trust me," said Quick.

The Indians slowed down when they neared the clearing. Quick's first count was forty. When the Indians discovered the bodies, they all rushed in to get a look. They exhibited much excitement.

Kathy Gale wanted a look. Handing the scope to her, she gasped at the large number and their excitement.

Handing the scope back to Quick, she asked, "Why are they so excited and seemingly out of control?"

"I can't tell you now, but some will be leaving."

CHAPTER 21: KILLING THE MEDICINE MAN

Taking back the scope, Quick located their medicine man, with his tall feathered staff and buffalo-horned headpiece. It seemed he was trying to settle down the war party, as some were leaving in the direction they had come.

Quick recognized the Indian he had released to give them his message. He was leading those leaving and was looking back, hollering at others. Quick handed Kathy Gale the scope so she could witness the exit of those leaving.

"You were right, Ryan. But how did you know?" asked Kathy Gale.

Quick estimated over half had left. The other half was being held back by the medicine man's pleadings and shaming. Now they were pointing at the four tethered mustangs. The Indians were afraid, and the four mustangs added to that fear. They thought it was a trap. But what kind of trap?

The medicine man apparently shamed their bravery until he convinced ten of them to go with him to retrieve the mustangs. When they reached the horses, four of them dismounted, untied the mustangs, jumped back on their horses, and raced back to the waiting group. The medicine man pranced around on his horse, hollering and shaking his staff toward the ranch house. Kathy Gale was in total shock and amazement when Quick jumped out the window, shaking his Henry at the Indians. The six remaining Indians and the medicine man charged. Quick's first shot went between the eyes of the medicine man, sending him lifeless to the ground.

Quick held up his hand, giving the peace sign to all Indians. The Indian now out front leading the charge raised his rifle to fire. Quick raised the Henry with one hand and fired. He, too, died with one bullet between his eyes. Quick continued holding his hand in the air as the other five stopped and loaded the medicine man and the other dead Indian on their horses and returned to those waiting. The bullet between the eyes of the medicine man was all the convincing the other Indians needed as to whose medicine was the strongest. They retreated to the southwest with the medicine man as proof as to why they had not continued the fight.

Kathy Gale was speechless. Was Ryan in cahoots with the Indians? Has he had past dealings with them? He must have to be able to predict their behavior. Still, she could not take her eyes off him. She did not want to be associated with a bounty hunter, especially one that had developed a relationship with the Comanche. When this was over, she would find someone more suitable and never give Ryan another thought.

"Kathy Gale, I feel we are safe for the time being but think we need to stay close to the cabin until the Texas Rangers have the time to stop all the raids. Is that all right with you?"

Kathy Gale was seated when Quick called her name and a good thing too. She did not want to use the "stump my toe" excuse for the weak knees and deep emotions she was having when he called her name.

Maybe I should ask him to go back calling me Miss Chambers, she thought, then Nooo! I like this feeling. I'll simply wait and decide until I get out of this situation and back to civilization.

"Kathy Gale, did you hear me?"

"Oh, yes, I think it would be best also. I don't know what I would do if I got burned out."

"Are you attached to this place?"

"No! Not at all, but it's all I've got, and I must take care of it," explained Kathy Gale. "I don't care much for the loneliness of the ranch or even ranching itself."

"Why don't you sell out and invest your money in banking or railroad stock?" suggested Quick. "I know of some good railroad stock that pays great dividends. A little investment would give you a very good income, and you could live anywhere you wanted. You should think it over."

Don't tell me I'm in love with a bounty-hunting, gunfighting, Indian-loving, con-man, am I? So! It's my money he's after. Wait! Did I say I was in love? Is this feeling I've been having love? Oh my!

"Ryan, why did they leave after you shot the medicine man and the other Indian attacking you?"

"The medicine man is the spiritual leader of the tribe. He takes care of their souls. He is an advisor to the chief on many matters. He usually never enters in battle but encourages the warriors in the direction they should go. He has much power and is followed unquestionably by the tribe with the chief 's consent. Apparently, the medicine man had lost face with many in the tribe and was trying to gain it back. After half of the warriors deserted him, after finding the four dead, he had to show his bravery by retrieving the four mustangs. He got caught up in his own bravery and attacked. Once I killed him, his strong medicine was gone and left them without a spiritual leader. They left in fear of the white man's medicine."

"Ryan, where did you learn all this? You seem to know what they would do before it happened."

"Kathy Gale, I do know a lot about Indians, and I will share everything with you at the right time. Now is not the right time. I want no one to know what happened here today. It is very important to me."

"Ryan, you should want everyone to know what happened here. You saved my life. You singlehandedly ran the Indians away. You know—"

"Kathy Gale!" Quick insisted. "Please trust me. My life and yours could be in the balance. I'm asking you, and I need an answer now. Will you not mention anything you have witnessed here these last two days?"

"I'm sorry, Ryan. Of course, I will not mention anything that's happened in the last two days."

Knowing that Echo would alert them of any danger and both being exhausted, they drifted off into a peaceful sleep. Echo again woke them. Looking out the window, Quick saw a small swirl of dust coming from the southeast. Could be just a dust devil? Quick thought. He felt refreshed and happy having Kathy Gale at his side. He thought they must have been asleep for several hours.

Kathy Gale was looking at him, smiling. "Ryan, I'm happy you are here with me."

Looking through his scope, he determined that the dust was coming in a straight line toward them. It wasn't a dust devil.

"We have company coming, Kathy Gale," warned Quick.

In less than five minutes, five riders spilled into the clearing from the southeast and were riding hard toward the cabin. It took a couple of minutes to locate the star on each. They were Texas Rangers!

Quick made that announcement then rushed to get his bedroll. He broke down the Henry and rolled it tightly inside the bedroll then placed the bedroll out of sight.

Kathy Gale did not know what to think. She was happy the Texas Rangers were here. What's going on in Ryan's mind? Is he afraid of the Texas Rangers? He is not afraid of Indians. Why should he be afraid of the Texas Rangers?

Quick saw the look in Kathy Gale's eyes and said, "Just trust me. If not, I will ride out now."

"I'll trust you, Ryan."

"Just let me handle everything," said Quick. "Let's go out and greet them." After moving to the front yard, they waved a vigorous welcome at the approaching riders.

All five were riding large, strong horses with no distinctive markings on any of them. Each carried a Winchester in their saddle scabbard and two Colt .45s. Quick assumed each also carried at least one hideout if not two.

The rangers spread out as they approached. It was difficult for Quick to determine their pecking order but identified their leader, soon enough. He sat tall in his saddle and was giving commands to his men with eye contact as they were riding in.

As he made his approach, he looked straight at Quick and with utmost authority, asked, "What's the situation here?"

Quick spoke, smiling. "Glad to see you, Captain, and your men."

"I'm Sergeant Cline, and I asked what is the situation here?"

"Everything is fine now you're here," explained Quick. "We thought that we were in for it. About forty Indians rode in from the southwest this morning around ten o'clock. Some left immediately, and the rest left shortly after, back to the southwest."

"What's your name, mister?" quizzed the sergeant.

"Ryan Riemens, and this is Miss Chambers. This is her ranch."

"You okay, ma'am?" the sergeant directed to Kathy Gale.

"Yes, of course," Kathy Gale said with a smile. "Would you get down and have some coffee while I fix us all something to eat?"

"Sure will, ma'am." Turning to one side, he told two to look around the barn and the other two to go to the southwest corner and look for signs.

Quick's mind raced. He had forgotten to wipe out the four mustangs' unshod hoof prints in the barn. In his mind, he ran through the two or three answers he would consider when confronted with questions based on the four men's report when they returned. Quick had learned a long time ago how hard it was to keep a story straight. The truth was always easy. He had to be careful because the last thing he would want to happen was to get crosswise with the Texas Rangers. He thought it best to lay out the story with Sergeant Cline.

He revealed that he had been chased by nine Comanche and that he had taken shots at them from over his shoulder. He told the sergeant about being on the lookout for a man that he thought might be in the area. He told him about his visit with Sheriff Sterling and informing him he would look in on Miss Chambers and make sure she was safe and would bring her back to San Angelo if the situation warranted it. He knew of the anticipated arrival of the Texas Rangers. He had discussed the situation with Miss Chambers. Both decided it would be best to wait it out here until the Rangers arrived, or they gave an all-clear that it would be safe for them to return to San Angelo unescorted.

"When the war party arrived, why didn't they attack you?" Sergeant Cline asked.

"I asked the same question, Sergeant. The only answer I could come up with was this ranch had a previous owner that killed many Comanche from five hundred to eight hundred yards with a Sharps buffalo gun. The Comanche had left this area for that reason. Some of the warriors might have remembered that, and it brought doubt and fear into their minds," clarified Quick. He continued, "Then, it could have been that I might have wounded or killed one or more of the nine Comanche, which were very important to the tribe. They may have only discovered that when they arrived and then decided to return the body or bodies to the tribe."

Quick, not knowing what or how much the sergeant might know, did see a slight change in the sergeant's attitude.

"You might be right on both counts," the sergeant said. "There could be as many as three hundred in the main party and are picking up stragglers on the way. They all seem to be in a hurry to get out of here."

Quick was very conscious of Kathy Gale hanging on to every word said. If she betrayed him, he would surrender peaceably rather than risking harm to her or any of the rangers. The two rangers inspecting the barn area reported seeing hoof- prints of unshod mustangs. Quick spoke up and said he saw four mustangs late last night in the barn scrounging for loose dropped grain.

They reported seeing no sign of Indians. The other rangers were heading in from the southwest. Quick was hoping that the blood, in the middle of the clearing, would not be seen. The two told Sergeant Cline they estimated from thirty-five to forty-five Indians in the party. They think something excited them. There was blood on the ground. Most was clotted and churned up by the many horses. Several of the Indians had dismounted and walked around the blood.

155

"Mr. Riemens, how many of those Indians did you hit when you were riding in?"

"I sure didn't take the time to count. It could have been only one or all of them. I was running for my life and trying to shoot them by shooting over my shoulder. I did not see any of them fall off their horses. I saw a couple of them duck after I shot. I think the two were hit, but I'm not sure," Quick explained. "I'm not a good shot, even facing someone, and shooting over my shoulder on a running horse would make me even a worse shot."

"If you're such a bad shot, you are in the wrong business," Sergeant Cline spoke up, "And what business is that? Bounty hunting?"

"Sir, I am not a bounty hunter. I just so happen to be hunting a man with a price on his head for a crime he didn't commit," Quick clarified. "I'm trying to find him before some real bounty hunter does and kills him before he can clear up his name."

"Well, Mr. Riemens, you must be crazy, or awfully brave, to ride in this country alone with over three hundred Comanche on the warpath," the sergeant stated.

"No, Sergeant, you and your men are the brave ones. Sheriff Sterling told me only twenty Texas Rangers were sent to put down the three hundred renegade Indians," Quick said. "I'll volunteer for being the crazy one. Hearing of Miss Chambers being here and her uncle having no desire to rescue her, I just couldn't stand by and not do anything. There was also a possibility of finding the person I've been looking for."

After eating, it was decided that all would spend the night and leave for San Angelo first thing in the morning. The sergeant assigned guard duties to the rangers. Quick told of Echo's ability as a sentry, and that he would be near.

Before daybreak, Kathy Gale was preparing breakfast as the others were preparing to leave. Quick reached out and touched Kathy Gale's arm and looked at her straight in the eyes.

"Thank you for everything, Kathy Gale."

Kathy Gale steadied herself with her other hand, "I'm trusting you," she whispered.

Sergeant Cline did not want to leave Kathy Gale's weapons in the ranch house for fear the Indians might raid them after they had left. Quick put the Sharps in his scabbard on his saddle and carried one of the Winchester rifles in his hand. Kathy Gale retrieved her personal Winchester and strapped on her Colt. The rest were bundled and put on one of the packhorses.

Chapter 22: Kathy Gale's Return to San Angelo

Three of the rangers spread out and spearheaded their rapid retreat toward San Angelo. As night approached and not having seen any fresh sign of Indians, they decided to make camp before dark.

Just at dark, a Texas Ranger messenger asked for permission to enter the camp. Granted, he rode in with one packhorse. He had orders for Sergeant Cline. The Comanche tribe was moving due west and was between the Concho and the Middle Concho rivers. They were picking up marauders along the way, adding to their group as they moved west. They were waiting for no one and had traveled all the previous night.

The Comanche were running from something, and it was not the Texas Rangers. Sergeant Cline and his troops were to join the pursuit and keep the Comanche heading due west toward the desolate plains, which had little water or vegetation.

The orders were to prevent the Comanche from going north into the plateaus and arroyos. By keeping them heading west, this would enable the rangers to fight at a distance. Many of the Comanche had no rifles. Of those that did, most were not good shots.

Sergeant Cline had to follow his orders and give chase. Quick and the sergeant agreed the Comanche had cleared out of the area they were in now. Both agreed they would have no interference from the Indians on their continued journey to San Angelo. The sergeant also pointed out that they probably would not see any white men either because they had no way of knowing that the area was cleared of Indians.

Early the next morning before sunup, a big breakfast was cooked by the rangers. Kathy Gale had wanted to help, but they graciously refused. They had fixed enough for everyone to have breakfast and enough for lunch and snacks. Quick and Kathy Gale's portions had been parceled together.

Sergeant Cline told Quick he needed only one packhorse, and he was leaving one for him to haul Kathy Gale's weapons. He was to turn the packhorse into the hostler in San Angelo and held there until his return. If agreeable, which it was, Sergeant Cline wanted all their unprepared foodstuffs. He would give them a voucher to replace them at the general store.

Quick and Kathy Gale thanked the rangers for their rescue and wished them luck. Both parties moved out.

Kathy Gale was excited to spend the day with Ryan. It was like attending dances with the music and happy faces all around. She had experienced numerous men flirting with her, holding her hand, some even trying to kiss her.

What she did not like was that her uncle Calvin had a rule that she could only dance two times with any boy or man. Never once did she ever have a romantic feeling with any of them. Some could dance better than others, and that was the ones she liked. Thus far, the time she had spent with Ryan alone was concentrated on their survival. Then the rangers had been with them for two nights and one day.

Kathy Gale did not know how she knew Ryan was the one. Was it because of the danger they had faced? Was it because he showed her he would protect her? She knew that he was the one, regardless of what he was. She had never wanted to kiss a man except for her father, and that didn't count. Now she was having all sorts of desires she never thought of before.

She knew that a lot of women spent their married life trying to change their husbands. They married them knowing what they were and didn't like it, but were convinced that they could change them. Everyone she knew failed and lived a miserable life fighting and arguing. She vowed never to try to change Ryan.

What she knew now was that he was intelligent. Much more than anyone she had ever known. He could think on his feet. He made plans and carried them out to perfection. He had shown instances of tenderness toward her and instances of firmness when required. Ryan never showed disrespect for her. The one thing that concerned her was he had never flirted or really showed signs that he was interested in her, like most of the boys she knew. It could be he was more man than a boy. It also concerned her that Ryan was more interested in the man he was chasing than her. Kathy Gale had always had to chase men away and had no clue how to act now that she had found the one.

Quick had suggested they ride side-by-side when the terrain permitted, and he would lead the packhorse. He also suggested that any conversation should be done in a low voice. Even though he did not expect others would be in the area, it did not alter his trained constant awareness of his surroundings.

After constant riding for four hours, Kathy Gale asked if they could stop for lunch.

"Sure," said Quick. "I would like that."

Kathy Gale spread her bedroll, and Quick spread the food prepared by the Texas Rangers. After eating, Kathy Gale asked, "Ryan, tell me what you can about yourself."

"Kathy Gale, I would never lie to you. I'm in a very precarious situation. I truly want to tell you everything about myself, but to do so, I would be placing a burden on you. I may never be able to tell everything. When I can, I assure you that you will be the first person I tell."

"I don't know how you could ever be a burden on me," reassured Kathy Gale.

"I will tell you a few things. I am well-read. I have a vast knowledge of self-defense, languages, geography, and psychology. I have no regrets about actions I've taken against others. I have no family, but I do have several loyal friends that also helped in my training. I do not know where they are now, but I'm sure my friends know of my precarious position and will show up to assist me. That is all I can tell you now. We need to move on if you want to reach San Angelo by nightfall."

Kathy Gale did not want to move on. She wanted to spend as much time alone with Ryan as possible. She wanted to spend one night on the trail alone with Ryan. Quick wanted to spend one night on the trail alone with Kathy Gale. Kathy Gale rode as slow as she could. Quick stopped several times and rearranged the pack on the packhorse. After moving on, Kathy Gale requested to stop for a rest.

While resting, Quick spoke up. "Kathy Gale, it will be after dark before we get to San Angelo. Why don't we pull up a couple hours before dark, make camp for the night, and freshen up for our entry into San Angelo in the morning? I really need to bathe and change clothes."

"Oh! I agree. These past few days have been stressful."

After finding a perfect place close to the Concho, the camp was made. Quick gathered stones and made a fire pit. He then took his saddlebag with his change of clothes and threw it over his shoulder. He told Kathy Gale to keep her Colt handy, and that Echo would alert them of any danger. He would be back shortly. She said she would go downstream and look for some ripe mustang grapes.

Quick went up the river one hundred and fifty yards. He removed his clothes and carried his two Colts, Henry, and a bar of soap into the stream waist-deep. He placed his weapons on a flat stone in the river and started scrubbing.

Kathy Gale watched him go until he was out of sight. She did not want to take her eyes off him. Starting down the river, Kathy Gale had only gone a few steps when she stopped. She decided she had better go up the river also to not get lost or get too far away from him, in case she needed protection. After walking quickly up the river, there was Quick standing in the water fifty yards upstream, facing the far bank. She had never seen a naked man before. She could see every muscle in his body. They were long and distinct. His skin was so tight, it made every muscle ripple with every move he made, making him look so graceful.

Shaking with excitement and fear of getting caught, she was well hidden in tall buffalo grass and other brush. This is so exciting, looking at his back.

Suddenly, Quick turned facing the near bank. Kathy Gale looked at his broad shoulders, and her eyes moved down his chest and stomach! Oh my!

Kathy Gale was glad she had the wind in her favor as she turned and ran away without being heard. She was embarrassed beyond belief. She never intended to see what she did. She prayed that Ryan had not seen her. Her happiness faded away with the fear that he had. If Ryan had seen her, she was going to tell him how she felt about him and plead for forgiveness or lie about seeing him. She now cared not if he was a bounty hunter, gunman, or con-man.

Ryan was the only man that ever made her feel the way she did and never wanted to be without this feeling. Kathy Gale waited at the camp with tears in her eyes. She did not know if they were tears of joy or tears of fear that Ryan would reject her. She was at a total loss as to what she should do.

Upon Quick's arrival, back at camp, he observed Kathy Gale busily placing wood in the fire pit. She looked up and saw the big grin on his face. Her mind raced. Had he seen her watching? Embarrassment flooded her body. She cowered away from him, trying to gain composure.

"Are you okay?" Quick asked.

Not looking at him, she answered, "Yes, I did not expect you back so soon and was slightly startled. I wanted to have the fire going before you returned and had my mind elsewhere when you showed up."

"Oh, hope I didn't interrupt a pleasant thought," said Quick.

She turned facing Quick wholly composed. "No, on the contrary. If okay with you, we would just eat jerky tonight. The fire is for the ambiance. There are things I need to share with you before we reach San Angelo and thought this would be a good time."

"Sounds good to me," Quick replied.

"Ryan, long as I can remember, Dad had me on a horse," Kathy Gale began. "It started with me riding the range, sitting in front of him, in the saddle. I had my own horse at the age of four. I had my own pistol at the age of five. I could not physically pull the trigger until the age of six. But every day, I practiced. At eight, Dad cut off the stock of one of his rifles. Even though I could not fire it, he required me to carry it with me around the ranch. He taught me the ranching business, the boundaries of the ranch, how to sell cattle, and how to determine if a cow was sick. Mother was fighting for her time to teach me to cook, sew, dance, read, and write."

Kathy Gale continued, "My mother died when I was ten years old. Father's brother never married. We only saw him when he was down on his luck. Then he would stay with us a couple of months, doing odd jobs around the ranch. Father would pay him cowboy wages. When my uncle accumulated a little money, he would leave. When he would come back, he was always broke. Mother did not like having him around. After she died, Uncle Calvin moved in permanently. He took numerous trips to San Angelo, staying in our townhouse while there. When he was at the ranch, he was good company for Father."

"My father was much older than Uncle Calvin and was in failing health," Kathy Gale explained. "Father thought I needed a broader education than I could get on the ranch and sent me to a boarding school in St. Louis shortly after Mother's death. I was there for two years. I loved it. Students from different states and countries attended. It was exciting." But Father's health worsened, and he wanted me home. I was only twelve years old when I arrived back."

"Father discussed with Uncle Calvin what was to happen upon his death. I listened but had no input. I was fourteen when Father died, and I inherited the ranch. Uncle Calvin was appointed my guardian until I was eighteen or married. Any sale of cattle had to have my name on the bill of sale. The money from each sale was to be deposited in the Ranchers Preferred Bank of San Angelo in my name. This had never been discussed with me or Uncle Calvin. Father knew Uncle Calvin had a gambling problem. He trusted Uncle Calvin with me but did not trust him with the money."

"I ran the ranch with the foreman and three hands. Uncle Calvin stayed in San Angelo and only showed up at the ranch to get money. He tried to gain access to the ranch funds with the probate judge but failed. I continued paying cowboy wages to Uncle Calvin as Father had done, but he was always asking for more money," Kathy Gale explained. "When I resisted, Uncle Calvin began hitting me until I gave in. I don't know why I didn't just give him the money before he hit me, but I didn't."

"I went to San Angelo escorted by my ranch foreman two months ago. I ran into my friend, Mary Jo Stubblefield and her family. They told me they had been looking for me. They were buying supplies for a trip to Waco and were leaving in three days. Mary Jo's mother and father wanted me to go along. They were going to a cousin of Mary Jo's wedding. It was going to be a big wedding with a lot of parties and dances. Her brother was insistent that I go. He had always paid me a lot of attention, but I was never interested in him, yet I wanted to go."

"Uncle Calvin would never give me permission to go, but I was determined to go anyway. I assured Mary Jo's parents that I would be happy to go and would be back in time for their designated departure."

"Rocky Lane, my foreman, escorted me back to San Angelo on the departure date and kept me out of Uncle Calvin's sight. I did not disclose to Rocky where I was going or who with, only that I would be back in two weeks."

"Mary Jo, Trey, and I rode horseback. Mr. and Mrs. Stubblefield rode in a two-horse buggy with room for the luggage and supplies," continued Kathy Gale. "Not wanting to be seen leaving town with the Stubblefield party, I waited and caught up to the group three miles down the road."

"We had been in Waco only three days when Uncle Calvin showed up. Just as Mary Jo, Trey, and I were leaving a dance, Uncle Calvin sucker-punched Trey and dragged me back to my room in the hotel. He had me change into my riding clothes. I left a note to Mary Jo, apologizing, and asking her to please take care of my luggage. I made one last attempt to stay. He needed money, and I was his only source. I offered him all I had if he would let me stay.

He laughed in my face. He told me he was taking all my money and would throw a rope around me and drag me back to the ranch if I did not saddle up and ride."

"We had no knowledge of the Comanche uprising until we rode upon a burning ranch house near the Star area, fifteen miles east of Goldthwaite. At my insistence, we stopped to bury a man and woman. I had my Colt on and had laid my Winchester aside. I had finished digging the first grave and had started the second when I saw three Indians riding in. I grabbed the Winchester and jumped in the grave. Uncle Calvin had beat me in and was lying in the bottom. I drew my Colt and started firing. I unseated the closest one with a shot in the chest. I wounded the second with a shot in the stomach. With my Colt empty, I switched to the Winchester and finished the first one off with the first shot. The third was now racing toward the mesquite a good two hundred yards off. I took my time and killed him with the first shot. Uncle Calvin had recovered from his prone position at the bottom of the grave. He emptied the pistol and Winchester fast and hit nothing. The first Indian was retreating because he probably thought he had ten people shooting at him."

"We moved through the Goldthwaite pass into the valley. The trading post at Goldthwaite had been abandoned and emptied. Below the horseshoe curve near the low-river crossing on the Colorado, we were attacked by a war party just as we crossed. There were quite a few dead Indians before the fighting broke off. Why they just quit, we don't know. They just disappeared. We left the area as fast as our horses would go. At my insistence, we changed to a slower pace. Uncle Calvin would have ridden the horses to their death. Then we would have really been in trouble. We worked our way to the ranch. Even though Rocky and the hands were gone, Uncle Calvin took all the money and left, headed back toward San Angelo. He left me at the ranch alone. I had told him I was afraid of a possible raid on the ranch. He said the Indians were in the Goldthwaite area and a long way from the ranch and dismissed my concerns."

Tears came into Kathy Gale's eyes as she looked away. "Him being my only relative, I sometimes think he wants me to get killed so he can inherit the ranch."

"Look out for him, Ryan! He will make something out of me leaving the ranch and you being alone with me during this trip. He prides himself of being a brawler, and he is an expert on delivering sucker punches."

"Kathy Gale, let me handle Uncle Calvin. I've figured him out. He preys on the weak, and the ones he thinks are weak. If he bothers you or me, I will try not to kill him, but he might wish he were dead."

"Ryan, do you think you could beat him in a hand-to-hand fight?"

"Kathy Gale, I don't know. But if he did beat me, he would have to do it every time he saw me, and I'm sure he would get tired of having to do that, so he would stay clear of me."

This brought a grin to Kathy Gale's face. "Ryan, do you think you would stay around for that possibility?"

"You can take that to the bank!" Quick replied.

This had been the first time there had been time for both to relax, smile, and talk. A lot of Kathy Gale's smiles were brought on by reflecting on her secret voyeurism of Ryan and the excitement and fear of being caught. She promised herself that she would never do that again.

A lot of Quick's smiles were brought on by being alone with Kathy Gale. The smiles were hampered by the thought of the bounty on his head and the necessity of clearing his name. He could not win

Kathy Gale's heart until she knew all the details of how and why he had the bounty on his head. It could be wishful thinking on his part, but he thought Kathy Gale was liking him a little. But he still had to play hard to get. He had made up his mind. Now that he had found her, he was not going to leave San Angelo without her. Uncle Calvin, bounty hunters, or Indians, it mattered not. He was not leaving!

Early the next morning, Kathy Gale heard two shots. She reached for her Winchester only to see Quick waving at her as he reloaded his Colts. She waved back. He was fifty yards away, walking back with two headless blue quail.

"When I woke up, I saw them running down the road and thought they would be mighty good for breakfast. I didn't want to lose them, so I shot them. I felt it would be safe to shoot them being this close to San Angelo. I'm sorry I woke you up."

"That's okay," said Kathy Gale.

"I'm not in a particular hurry, and if you're not, just lay back, and I'll fix the quail," said Quick.

"I could get used to this pampering," said Kathy Gale.

Quick bit his tongue to keep from saying he would pamper her for the rest of her life and said instead, "Everyone needs some pampering some of the time."

Kathy Gale threw her arms around her breast, squeezed, and thought, I think he likes me.

Quick and Kathy Gale rode into San Angelo around 10:00 am. Several of Kathy Gale's friends greeted her along the way and expressed their happiness that she was safe. Each had cast an inquisitive eye toward Quick. Some knew of the bounty hunter, and it reflected in their mannerisms. He was introduced as Mr. Riemens, her rescuer.

Kathy Gale led the way to her townhouse, which was a mile due south of the town in a grove of cottonwood. Kathy Gale stopped to see if Uncle Calvin was there. She was not ready for the conflict that she knew would happen when Ryan and her uncle did meet. She uttered a sigh of relief when she saw he was not there.

A small spring creek ran from the back of the house to the rear of the barn. The barn was twice as big as the house. Both dismounted and tied off their horses. Kathy Gale reached out and touched Quick's arm.

"Quick, would you stay with me until the conflict I will have with Uncle Calvin is over?"

"Kathy Gale, I'll stay here until you run me off. I will never again let Calvin lay a hand on you. I'm telling you now if he tried in my presence, I would probably kill him."

Kathy Gale new that most western men, even outlaws, would not let a woman be abused, but what she just heard was different. It was so definite and adamant.

Quick reached out and grasped her arm. "Don't worry, I will be here."

CHAPTER 23: CONFLICT WITH UNCLE CALVIN

The news of Kathy Gale's safe arrival spread, along with the news that the bounty hunter, Ryan Riemens, rescued her. The news that Kathy Gale had shown up safely was a small disappointment to Calvin. That she was with a man, and that man was Ryan Riemens was enough to force him away from the gaming table.

Calvin felt he must discourage any possible interest Mr. Riemens might have for Kathy Gale. He would falsely express his thanks and gratitude for the rescue of his niece, then dismiss Mr. Riemens.

As he was rounding the corner of the road, he saw Quick removing his hand from Kathy Gale's arm. Calvin, having no visible weapon, felt secure and thought that he could use this as an excuse to provoke a fight with this bounty hunter, without firearms being involved. His thoughts were that even though Riemens was taller, he was much thicker and seemingly stronger. He felt he could physically demolish the young Mr. Riemens and belittle him in the eyes of Kathy Gale.

Calvin rushed up and got in Quick's face, raising his arms and shouting that Quick was never to touch his niece again and to get out and never come back. While this was going on, Quick slowly moved his right hand to the middle of Calvin's chest. Without touching him, Quick moved his head down, looking at Calvin's chest. Calvin stopped his verbal assault and could not resist looking down. Quick gently raised his hand, hooking Calvin under the nose and raised his hand until Calvin's head tilted back. Quick was smiling, and Kathy Gale broke into hilarious laughter. Calvin was speechless.

Quick suggested that they start the conversation over. Calvin agreed in a calmer voice. He relaxed and seemed to turn away from Quick, then turned back with a vicious back-arm swing at Quick's head. Quick also turned in the same direction, ducked, and grabbed Calvin's arm as it flew past him and kept pulling it in the same direction. Quick then pulled down on Calvin's arm, sending him flying over his head and crashing him to the ground on his back. This knocked the wind out of Calvin.

Not wanting to kill Calvin, Quick straddled him, then placed his right knee in Calvin's solar plexus and set down. He pulled the knee up so Calvin could breathe. Each time Calvin got his wind back and acted as if he wanted to fight, Quick would simply rock forward on his right knee, again forcing all the air out of Calvin's lungs. This left Calvin beating the ground, trying to get his wind back. After the third time, Calvin realized he was trapped. The only thing he could do was lie still and keep quiet. Quick then placed his knees on top of Calvin's outstretched arms and leaned forward on his knees to take the pressure from Calvin's chest. Quick slapped Calvin's face several times to steady his breathing. Calvin tried to free his arms several times, and all Quick had to do was rock forward, putting more weight on his arms with his knees. Kathy Gale stood by silently in total awe of what just happened to Uncle Calvin.

Quick spoke up. "Calvin, I wanted to have a civil conversation with you. Now that I've met you, this is the best time and place to have it."

"Now let me up!" cried Calvin.

"No! I don't want to hurt you or kill you. This is the safest place for you. You are going to stay where you are and listen to me."

"No, I'm not!" Calvin shouted.

Quick reached out with his left hand and grabbed a handful of hair from the back of Calvin's head and pulled it forward. As he was doing this, he placed the heel of his right hand under Calvin's nose and pushed up gently. Calvin released a terrifying scream. Quick released Calvin's hair and nose and said, "Where were we, Calvin? Oh, yes, you were going to lie here and listen to me."

A feeble "okay" was uttered from Calvin's mouth.

"First thing, Calvin, you can forget about me leaving here. I will stay here as long as I like."

Calvin said in a calm voice, "If you will let me up, I will change your mind about that."

Quick rocked up on Calvin's arms and said, "OK, I will remove your hideouts, and I'll let you up to see if you can change my mind. Calvin, you have no clue what you are asking for."

A fast search revealed a Dillinger in his coat pocket and another in his waistband. Throwing the Dillingers to the side, Quick said, "Calvin, I told you I did not want to hurt or kill you. I will try not to kill you, but you will be hurt, and you might die."

Calvin was eager to get off his back and take care of this young fool. As young as Riemens was, Calvin thought that he would not be able to handle all his tricks. He thought Riemens's words were just that, words. This bounty hunter had gotten lucky the first time. He had not taken advantage of having him pinned to the ground and had not hurt him in any way. He doubted if Riemens really knew how to hurt someone without shooting them.

Quick released Calvin and backed away, waiting to see what tactic he would come up with. Calvin got to his feet and rushed Quick with his head lowered with the intention of overpowering him. Quick also rushed in standing upright and kicked Calvin with all his might between his thighs. This brought about the anticipated results of Calvin's head snapping back, and both his hands reaching for his testicles and letting out a loud scream. While Calvin's head was tilted back, Quick closed his elbow and moved it back with his shoulder then while stepping forward, he shot the elbow into the screaming mouth. Blood and shattered teeth went out in all directions, and the force of the blow landed Calvin on his back. Looking down, it was evident that the nose had also been broken. Quick picked up both of Calvin's legs and rolled him on his side to keep him from drowning in his own blood. Calvin lay unconscious, still grasping his testicles.

Quick turned to Kathy Gale, who was standing wide-eyed and silent. "Kathy Gale, I need to continue my conversation with Calvin. I don't expect any more fight out of him, and I have a plan on how to handle this. We don't have time to discuss this but trust me, you will understand by the time I'm finished. If there is anything you disagree with, we can work it out in private."

Things were moving along so fast Kathy Gale's emotions were rampant. She reached out and touched Quick's arm. "I do trust you, Ryan. I've seen a lot of fights before. In all of them, people were mad at each other, hollering and shouting as they fought. How can you be so calm with Uncle Calvin attacking and shouting at you?"

"You can't think when you're mad, screaming, and shouting. Thanks for trusting me, Kathy Gale. I'm going to pull Calvin into the barn. Would you take the two Dillingers in the house and hide them, then bring me some wet rags back to the barn? I don't know how long it will take for Calvin to regain consciousness, but I want you to be here when he does. I want you to hear the conversation."

Kathy Gale returned with several wet towels and pulled Quick aside and whispered, "In the top soup bowl."

Quick started cleaning Calvin's battered face. The cool, wet towel created an immediate moaning response from Calvin. Still lying on his side, Calvin curled into a fetal position and grasped his testicles and leaned his head back. The moaning increased, and the flow of blood decreased from his mouth. Quick did not rush him into a conversation but let him continue his moaning. Finally, the blood flow and the moaning slowed. Quick waited another fifteen minutes, then spoke with authority, "Calvin, I'll give you five more minutes to stop moaning, then we will continue our conversation."

Calvin opened his eyes, and for the first time, fear seemed to ravage his whole body. He immediately closed them to regain control of his emotions. He was nauseated. The kick to the testicles was what made him so sick. At this point, he did not think of his broken teeth.

"OK, your five minutes are up, stop all the moaning. I will start over with our conversation unless you want to start over with the fight. Your choice. Which will it be?"

Calvin couldn't get his answer out fast enough. "Conversation."

"You can forget about me leaving. I will stay here as long as I like. Since I like it here, I will be staying a long time," Quick began. "Calvin, you have shown no concern for your niece. Leaving her at the ranch with an Indian uprising in the area and showing no effort to rescue her led me to believe you might want her dead. It's my understanding that you have been taking money from her that you did not have coming. I don't want that to ever happen again. Do you understand?"

174

With a slurred response, Calvin got out that he did not think that was any of his business.

"I'll just put my dog in the hunt and make it my business. On top of the money, I have seen you hit her in anger. If you ever hit her again, I will kill you."

"That's a lie. No one has ever seen me strike Kathy Gale!"

"Calvin, I should kill you now for calling me a liar. I will let it go for now, but because of this new development, you have twenty-four hours to get out of town and forty-eight hours to get out of the state. I'll buy you a horse and will bring him around in less than an hour. After forty-eight hours, if I ever see you again, I will kill you."

"Kathy Gale, come with me."

It was obvious to Kathy Gale that Uncle Calvin had crossed the line by calling Quick a liar, as it was with most Texans. In doing so, any other Texan would have taken immediate action, armed or not. She expected it from Quick. She was confused with his lack of response. Why would he lie about seeing Uncle Calvin hitting her? She knew no one who was ever around when he would hit—her heart raced before finishing the thought. The man on the cliff?

If it were, why had he not told me? Why all the secrecy concerning Ryan?

She hated Uncle Calvin for all the things he did to her but did not want to be involved with anyone that killed him. Is this why Ryan did not kill him for calling him a liar? She knew Ryan was defending himself in the fight, and after seeing him shoot and fight, she knew Ryan could kill him at his will, but chose not to. Ryan had told her he was well-schooled in self-defense. Were the people that trained him a gang of bounty hunters? Was Ryan in cahoots with some of the Indians? Did Ryan follow her from the cliff? If so, why? Was Ryan after her ranch?

Just as they reached the front of the house, all the unanswered questions overwhelmed her. She could not control the tears that flowed down her cheeks or the sobs that were getting louder. Hearing the sobs, Quick turned and gently put his arms around her. "Kathy Gale, it's okay to cry. You've seen and been through a lot these last few days. I want you to know that you are safe with me and will remain so, as long as you wish."

Quick's arms tightened, and Kathy Gale responded with the tightening of her arms.

"Oh, Ryan, I'm sorry, I've had so many questions and received so many vague answers. I know you are busy now, but I have two questions that I must have answers for now."

"If I know the answers, you shall have the answer."

"Was it you on the cliff?"

"Yes, and I started to kill Calvin after he hit you."

"Why did you follow us?"

"Because I had fallen madly in love with you and had to find you."

Sobs turned into tears of joy as his embrace tightened.

"I know that I have fallen madly in love with you also, Ryan."

Passionate kisses seized the moment. Quick knew he had to get back to business.

"Kathy Gale, I must continue with my plan with Calvin. If all goes well, I will fill you in on all the secrets this afternoon. I am going to do everything in my power to completely win your heart. If after I tell you everything going on in my life, and you don't want to be a part of it, I will understand, but it will not diminish my love for you."

"Just the little bit I know about you now, Ryan, is enough for me to know that there could be nothing that would or could make me not want to be with you forever."

"Okay! Ready to go to work, Kathy Gale?"

"Of course. I will follow your lead."

"Let's get everything off the packhorse and set it inside. We will turn the packhorse into the hostler then go see Sheriff Sterling and discuss the situation we have with Calvin. Then we will go back to the livery and buy a horse for him."

"I'm sure Uncle Calvin has his horse stabled at the livery," said Kathy Gale.

"I'm sure it has your brand on it, Kathy Gale, and I'd rather buy him a horse than have him riding all over the country with a horse that has your brand on it."

Sheriff Sterling saw Quick and Kathy Gale going toward his office and headed them off. "Glad to see you both. Heard you were in town and was going just now to look you up. Come on down to the office with me. Any luck in finding Quick Tender?"

Kathy Gale looked up and thought, *that's a strange name, but I like it. Is that who Ryan has been looking for?*

"Saw some of his sign and felt close several times, but I put him on the back burner while dodging Comanche and looking out for Kathy Gale. Five Texas Rangers showed up the next day after I got to Kathy Gale's ranch. We thought the ranch house would be an easier place to defend ourselves than being on the trail trying to get here. We decided it best to wait for the rangers, and it worked out fine. The rangers escorted us back to a safe distance to San Angelo, then we came in alone. The rangers left with orders from a messenger for them to give chase to the main tribe, moving west."

"Sheriff, I need to report an incident that occurred at Kathy Gale's townhouse."

Quick gave details of Calvin attacking him and Calvin taking money from Kathy Gale and hitting her numerous times. Quick gave the opinion that Calvin wanted Kathy Gale dead so he could inherit the ranch. He told Sheriff Sterling that with his and Kathy Gale's approval, he would like to stay in the barn at the townhouse for a couple of days and nights."

"Oh yes," Kathy Gale replied. "I would feel much safer."

"Kathy Gale, you might feel much safer staying in the hotel or one of your friend's townhouses," said the sheriff.

"I'm sure the hotel is booked solid with the uprising crowd," said Kathy Gale.

"May I speak with you alone for a few moments?" asked Sheriff Sterling.

Quick stood up. "I understand, Sheriff. I think you should speak to her alone. I'll be outside, Kathy Gale."

"Kathy Gale, I like Mr. Riemens. He is very polite, considerate, and competent. I have a lot of questions about him. How did he achieve these traits at such an early age? What's between him and Quick Tender?"

"Who is Quick Tender, Sheriff? I heard you mention him before."

Sheriff Sterling told Kathy Gale everything he knew about Quick Tender, ending with he was not sure but thought that Tender was innocent in the Cole brothers' murder charge. He wanted Kathy Gale to know that Mr. Riemens introduced himself as a bounty hunter in search of Quick Tender and that he was known around town as a bounty hunter. He just wanted her to think of her reputation.

Kathy Gale was in total shock but concealed it well. With the shooting between the eyes of the Cole brothers, the two gamblers in Salado, the Indians in Goldthwaite, and the ones at the ranch, there was no doubt in her mind that Ryan Riemens was Quick Tender.

"Sheriff, my life is worth much more than my reputation. Mr. Riemens has saved my life on possibly three occasions. He has been nothing but polite and respectable to me, and I want his protection."

"Then I am positive you will be in good hands," said Sheriff Sterling.

CHAPTER 24: CALVIN COMMITS MURDER

As soon as Calvin was sure Riemens and Kathy Gale had left, he pulled himself together. He sought out the hidden Colt .45 he had hidden in the barn months ago. The Colt and box of shells were found where hidden, wrapped in a watertight oilcloth. Not wanting to be seen in his current physical condition, he retreated to the back of the barn and followed the creek to the Concho. He crossed the Concho upstream from the creek by walking on stepping-stones and came out behind the buildings across the river. He kept to the back of the houses going west until he came up behind the one he often frequented.

Calvin tapped out the rhythmic knock he always used. He had previously always come at night, which made Consuela hesitant to open the door. Calvin knocked again, and she eased open the door and barely recognized Calvin with his blackened eyes, broken nose, and teeth. Before Consuela could say a word, Calvin slurred out, "Find Edgardo and bring him to me, here."

Consuela, realizing the urgency in the tone of Calvin's voice, left immediately to find her cousin, Edgardo Garcia del Toro.

Edgardo and Consuela had long ago disgraced their family's name: Consuela, with provocative and promiscuous behavior, now prostitution, and Edgardo with drinking, fighting, gambling, and numerous accusations of murder, mostly with knives.

Edgardo fled to Mexico, where he continued these practices and added robbery when he ran out of his family's money. The Mexican Federales ran him out of Mexico and back to Texas. He had been hiding out with Consuela, the only family member that would have anything to do with him. Within the hour, Consuela returned with news that Edgardo was coming in through the mesquite and would be here shortly. Calvin handed Consuela five silver dollars and told her to leave and not come back until tomorrow morning. Calvin sat impatiently, waiting for Edgardo.

Calvin had met Edgardo numerous times when visiting Consuela. He knew of all the rumors and personally knew his prestigious family. He and Edgardo had shared tequila on many occasions, and Calvin had discussed with him his many misdeeds.

Edgardo was well educated, and the thing he missed most was educated conversations. He had much pride in his knife-fighting ability, and it was rumored he would torture his opponent, mostly uneducated peons, by inflicting so many wounds that they would eventually bleed out. Edgardo knew of Calvin's difficulty in getting family money, especially now that Kathy Gale controlled all the purse strings. He could relate to that.

Calvin had been looking out the back window and opened the door just as Edgardo appeared. Without giving Edgardo time to ask, Calvin told him he had been beaten by four cowboys over a card game. Calvin had two glasses and a bottle of tequila set out. He poured each a shot.

He told Edgardo he had been wronged by his brother by not giving him an even share of the ranch with Kathy Gale. He complained that she demanded he work for every dollar she gave him. After several more shots of tequila and small talk from Edgardo about being able to relate to his problem, Calvin laid five one-hundred bills on the table, "I want her killed tonight. There is a young man with her that I also want to be killed. He's there just trying to get her money and should not be a problem for you. He's still wet behind the ears." Calvin continued, "I will pay you another five hundred tonight when you return from doing the job. I want you to kill the young man first, with a knife. Just slide it in under the heart."

"Don't be telling me how to kill someone with a knife," Edgardo shouted back to Calvin.

"Wait, you have not heard all of it yet," continued Calvin. "After you kill the man, I want you to strangle the girl, tear off all her clothes, and rape her. Put the knife in her hand and roll the kid on top of her."

With a big smile, Edgardo readily agreed.

"Let's have another shot." Grinning, Calvin added, "Oh! I forgot to tell you she's a virgin."

Quick and Kathy Gale returned with the horse for Uncle Calvin. Uncle Calvin was gone. Quick told Kathy Gale that he did not fear Uncle Calvin returning. "He will probably try to find someone to kill us," said Quick. He assured Kathy Gale he would and could defend her.

"I know," she said with a smile.

"Let's go into the house and make sure he is not in there," said Quick. When they discovered Calvin was not there, Quick told Kathy Gale he was going to trail him.

Quick put on his moccasins and said, "I'll be back shortly. Latch all the doors and pull in the string until I get back. I will be on foot, and I will leave Echo loose and command him to stay close. You are to stay inside. Keep your Colt in hand, and do not let anyone enter but me. I will signal you when I return."

"Okay, please hurry back. We have a lot of talking to do." Said Kathy Gale.

"Right!" said Quick. He smiled, thinking about Kathy Gale's last statement. He knew she knew of the danger they faced and was depending on him without questions or arguments.

Calvin's trail was easy to follow. He picked it up immediately, and a blind man could have followed it. The trail was secluded and was heading straight to the Concho. Quick headed upstream, a Calvin had and crossed the river using the same stepping-stones. Calvin's prints were the last made on the trail and made it easy to follow. Instead of following the exact trail, Quick moved off the trail for more cover and froze in his tracks when a Mexican woman rushed out of the back door of the third house west of the Concho and headed west on the trail. When she was out of sight, Quick hugged close to the houses on the north of the trail, moving up to and keeping out of the view from the window of the third house. He saw Calvin's tracks where he had stood outside the door.

The woman had disturbed the ground as she was leaving the door. Quick went back to the Concho and headed south, never losing sight of the door of the third house. He then turned west and moved past the fifth house and moved back north to the trail. There were no tracks of Calvin to be seen. He moved east past the fourth house, none there. Now he knew where Calvin was unless he had gone out the front door. He discounted that. Why would Calvin slip in the back door trying to not be seen then leave out the front door? He wouldn't, Quick concluded.

Quick again headed for the mesquite and backtracked his way back to the townhouse. His moccasins had left only a few markings, and Quick covered them as he went.

Kathy Gale let Quick in upon his return. He told her what he had found and surmised that Calvin had been looking for someone to kill him and/or both of them.

"I think if we are attacked, the attacker or attackers will come from the same house and follow the same trail. This is great knowledge to have," shared Quick.

"Which house was it, Ryan?"

"Third house on the left, west of the Concho."

"Consuela Toro! I know of her, Ryan. It is presumed she is a prostitute," declared Kathy Gale, "I know Uncle Calvin has spent a lot of time with her for the last twenty-five years." Kathy Gale continued. "Her extended family owns over one hundred thousand acres around Buffalo Gap, southwest of Abilene. They are wealthy and well respected in the area. Consuela was disowned by the family when what she had been doing for fun, she started doing for money. Not that she needed it. She has a cousin named Edgardo Garcia del Toro. He, for years, terrorized the Mexican communities with knife fights. After the family disowned him, the law clamped down on him and ran him off to Mexico. He had been there for over a year. It is rumored that he's been back for about three months and is hiding out with Consuela."

"Good to know, Kathy Gale. Nothing will happen until dark," said Quick. "Even then, it should be after midnight. Echo will alert of any danger. I've so much to tell you that I want to get started now."

Quick braced himself against the table, "Kathy Gale, please let me tell you the whole story about me, then I will answer all your questions."

"I will, Ryan."

It took five hours for Quick to tell the story because he not only told the story but expressed his thoughts, worries, and emotions, especially those concerning Kathy Gale. There were several interruptions by Kathy Gale's sobs and crying spells, but not one question did she ask. He left nothing out but his wealth. He did not know himself the vastness of such. He had laid out his plan to her, how he was going to clear his name, but could not tell her the timing. "OK, Kathy Gale, what are your questions?"

"None!" she replied.

Quick took her in his arms and told her he had a question. "Kathy Gale, as soon as I clear my name, will you marry me?"

Tears of joy filled her eyes. "Quick, I will marry you now, and we will clear your name later."

"Kathy Gale, you called me Quick. It sounded so good to me, but it could get me killed."

"I know. I just wanted to say it one time. As much as I love your name, I promise I'll never use it again until it's safe..., Ryan."

Neither was hungry, but they did eat some jerky.

"Kathy Gale, it's dark enough for me to slip out without being seen. Like I said earlier, I don't expect any trouble until around midnight. There are things I need to prepare for."

Quick sought one last hug before going out but received ten.

"I want you to know I am confident that we will be attacked from along the creek in the rear of the barn. I want you to stay inside without any fire or light. Check and place all your weapons, so you can find them in the dark, and don't forget the two Dillingers. Don't leave the house, and don't let anyone in but me. I'll knock 1-1-1," Quick explained between hugs. "I may bring the attacker in the house with me. If I do, I will knock 2-2-2. I'll give you one minute to get out of sight after you unlatch the door. I love you, Kathy Gale."

"Not as much as I love you," said Kathy Gale as she gave Quick one last hug as he slipped out the door.

Kathy Gale closed the door, dropped the latch, and pulled in the string. After checking and strategically placing her weapons, Kathy Gale piled all her pillows along the wall behind the bed, climbed in, and leaned against the pillows with her Winchester at her side. She then started planning her life with Quick Tender.

She figured with the ranch, and what money Quick might have, they might have enough saved to buy a store of some kind in town and live there. She thought of kids, at least five. They had the townhouse they could add on to as needed. She thought of cooking three meals a day and things she could do to keep Quick happy. Kathy Gale dreamed of schooling for the kids and grandbabies. She could not wait to share her thoughts with Quick.

Quick had already climbed a tall cottonwood tree and trimmed all the limbs below and to the west of him to give him the vision he anticipated needing. The attacker would be coming down the trail from the west and would have to pass under the cottonwood. Quick had tied three ropes in the tree and had rolled and placed them. He took one and descended to the ground. He picked up all the trimmings and disposed of them in the mesquite east of the barn.

Quick needed to know how many attackers would be coming from Consuela's house. His best bet on that was to see how many crossed the Concho and turned south. He did not have to see them but hear them. He decided to ride Echo bareback within earshot of the stepping stones and wait. He would be less than three hundred yards from Kathy Gale and would hear any shots, and with Echo, he could be there in a short amount of time. After determining the number of attackers, Quick would ride back to the cottonwood, grab the rope, and climb back up the tree. Then he would put Echo back on alert and be only fifty yards from Kathy Gale.

Quick rode west and made the northern turn up the Concho and stopped when he heard the water rushing past the footstones. Quick moved Echo off the trail back into the mesquite and turned back toward the footstones. Quick thought he was there way too early. It was only around ten-thirty. Echo stiffened slightly. Quick had not seen or heard anything. Echo had not changed his posture. All of a sudden, Quick saw one of the coal oil lights strung up along the street go out then reappear. Then he saw another. Someone was walking down the stepping stones blocking out the lamp as they passed.

Quick looked behind to see if there were others. There was none. He could now hear the man turning south along the Concho. He was only about thirty feet from Echo. Quick leaned forward and reached around Echo and grabbed his mane. He lowered his body to Echo's left side, and only his moccasin-covered foot was hanging over Echo's back. Echo snorted, and the man stopped and only saw the right side of Echo move off slowly toward the east. When out of sight of the man, Quick moved back on top of Echo and headed to the cottonwood. When reaching the tree, Quick grabbed the rope and left Echo's back without touching the ground. He had Echo move out four yards east of the tree and stand and face the incoming man from the west. Quick settled in and got two of the ropes ready if needed.

Quick heard him before he saw him. He was whispering, in Spanish, to Echo to calm him. Quick could not make him out before he got directly under him. He was still and silent. Quick looked for movement or sound from others. There was none. Quick's plan was to throw the rope, secure both arms, pull him off his feet, tie him off to the limb, then draw his Colt from his belly, and look for any movement or sounds. If none, he would drop to the ground behind him, stripping his hands of any weapons. He would then tie his hands and feet from behind with pig ties and search him all over for all weapons in less than one minute. He accomplished all in forty-five seconds. Quick had found two Colts, two large throwing knives, one pick, and a carving knife.

Quick cut the rope holding the Mexican in the tree, letting him fall to the ground. Edgardo started to speak. "Silencioso, senor!" Quick said.

Speaking in a hushed tone, Edgardo said, "I speak English as well as you."

Quick slid Edgardo's two Colts behind his belt in the back and gathered his four knives and held them in his right hand. He reached down with his left and hooked him under the arm and dragged him on the ground to the door of the house where Kathy Gale waited inside.

After tapping on the door, Quick heard the latch raise. After a full minute, Quick entered, pulling Edgardo in with him. As prearranged, Kathy Gale was out of sight. While Edgardo was still on the floor, Quick checked all the ties and ropes, making sure Edgardo was securely tied. He then picked him up and placed him in a chair.

"Mr. Edgardo Garcia del Toro, I presume," stated Quick.

Edgardo became motionless with rage. He had been betrayed by Calvin Chambers.

"Well, Mr. Toro, you are Mr. Toro, aren't you?" goaded Quick.

"Yes," Edgardo retorted.

"Let's see how much Mr. Calvin Chambers paid you for killing me and his niece," said Quick while reaching into Edgardo's top shirt pocket. He pulled out five hundred dollars.

Quick laughed. "Only two hundred and fifty dollars each? He was going to pay you more when you got the job done, wasn't he, Mr. Toro?"

"Yes, another five hundred dollars," spat Edgardo.

"Are you telling me, the greatest knife fighter in the world would take on the second-best knife fighter in the world for only five hundred dollars?

"Who are you?" Edgardo asked.

"Oh, he didn't tell you? I'm the guy that beat him half to death over money," replied Quick. "I will tell you what I'm going to do, Mr. Toro. I'm going to take this five hundred dollars and give it back to his niece since that's where it came from. Also, Mr. Toro, instead of me killing you, I think I will just turn you loose. I don't think you would have tried to kill me if you had known how easy it would be for me to kill you. You can go back and collect the other five hundred from Mr. Chambers so this won't be a total loss to you."

Quick continued, "If you want this five hundred dollars, you are welcome to come back any time. No use to slip in because you can't. Just knock on the door. Now let me get you untied. I do insist you follow all my instructions. Understood?"

"Yes," said Edgardo begrudgingly.

"Okay, don't make any sudden moves. Okay, Mr. Toro? This won't take long," Quick stated while loosening Edgardo's binds. "I relieved two Dillingers from Mr. Chambers, and he left before I could return them. Would you mind returning them for me?"

"No, not at all," sneered Edgardo.

"Now let me pull the table over in front of you. I'm going to give your knives back since I hear you are so fond of them. Now don't reach for them because you might lose a finger if you tried."

After laying the four knives on the table, Quick told him he had to get the two Dillingers out of a bowl on the top shelf. As Quick turned and was reaching for the bowl, Edgardo reached for one of the throwing knives. Before it rose from the table, Quick threw his knife, backhanded, with his left hand, and severed Edgardo's middle

189

finger on his right hand. Edgardo screamed and grabbed his right hand with his left.

In less than a second, Quick was behind Edgardo with a knife to his throat,

"Mr. Toro, settle down. You do not want to die, do you?"

"No! Where did that knife come from?" Edgardo screamed.

"I had told you not to reach for your knife, that you might lose a finger. Now, do you want to reach again and lose another finger?"

Edgardo scowled at Quick while uttering a low "No!"

"Okay, let me stitch up where the finger was and get you bandaged up," Quick offered as he removed all the knives from Edgardo's reach and got to work.

After an hour and a pint of tequila, Edgardo's bleeding and pain had diminished. While cleaning the table, Quick flipped the severed finger to Edgardo and asked, "Want this as a souvenir?"

Edgardo caught it and threw it back at him. Quick had moved aside and shot the finger out of the air two feet from Edgardo's hand. He had holstered his gun before Edgardo knew what had happened.

"I think you had better leave, Mr. Toro, before you get yourself killed. Here's another pint of tequila to help with the pain."

Quick slipped another round in his Colt, then unloaded Mr. Toro's two Colts and put his knives back from where he had taken them. He handed Edgardo the two Dillingers after loading one of them.

"I loaded one in case you come on a snake that needs killing. Don't forget what I told you about coming back. If you have Mr. Chambers' money, you are welcome anytime," Quick reminded Edgardo. "Mr. Toro, I'm going to walk out with you. I want you to walk back to the stepping-stones on the Concho, cross, and go straight to Consuela's house. Don't wander. If you do, I will kill you on the spot."

As they stepped out the door, Edgardo looked back. Quick had disappeared. After waiting ten minutes, Quick was sure that Edgardo would follow his instructions and meet up with Calvin. Edgardo would not only want the five-hundred dollars supposedly waiting for him, but he also wanted revenge.

Quick went back to the door and knocked lightly. The latch was lifted immediately. Quick entered and dropped the latch. Kathy Gale's arms were shaking. Not from fear, but from holding aim at Mr. Toro from the moment he was dragged in.

She fell into Quick's arms. "Why did you take so many chances with him, Ryan?"

"I didn't take any chances. I had a plan, and I knew exactly what he would do."

"Were you aiming at the second joint of his middle finger?"

"Of course, I knew I could hit it with a gun, and at close range, I am even more accurate with a knife. I only shot Edgardo's finger out of the air to show him I was as fast with a gun, so he would have an extra incentive to leave us alone."

"Kathy Gale, help me clean this mess up. I have things to do outside, then Echo and I will spend the rest of the night in the barn. Change the knock code to 3-1-3."

When finished, Quick went to the door. "See you early in the morning."

"Give me a hug," Kathy Gale said.

After several minutes, Quick eased out the door, leaving Kathy Gale to drop the latch.

Kathy Gale squeezed herself to make sure she was not dreaming all this, then dropped the latch and checked to make sure the string was in. She then leaned back against the door, smiled, and squeezed herself again.

Quick went to the cottonwood, climbed up the dangling rope, and untied all three and dropped them to the ground. He climbed down the tree, coiled the ropes, carried them to the barn, and tied them strategically from the crown and lofts. He loved swinging on ropes.

The throbbing in Edgardo's finger eased as the tequila he drank increased, but he was furious. Chambers had lied to him. Chambers knew how tough the kid was, and he should have told him. The kid proved to Edgardo that he did not ever want to mess with him again. Not even in a gang or ambush. He had lost the money Chambers had given him. He had lost most of his middle finger, and he never saw the girl that made this job sound so good.

Edgardo also knew Chambers would be furious and demand his money back. He thought the best way out of this was to tell Chambers that he was successful in completing the job, as he instructed. He would tell Chambers that he had lost his finger by some bad luck and for him not to worry about it. He thought the blood on him was enough to have come from three people, and he would act as the survivor. He also would throw in some comments about how pleasurable the rape was. After getting the rest of the money from Chambers, he would kill him. And Chambers deserved to be killed for lying about the kid being wet behind the ears. That lie cost him his finger and nearly his life.

Edgardo fixed a sling for his right hand to conceal the Dillinger that was loaded. His trigger finger was not injured and could pull the trigger when he reached for the money. He was ready.

Edgardo's tap on the back door of Consuela's house created a speedy response from Calvin. He was ready. He opened the door, letting Edgardo in.

"It's done!" Edgardo blurted out with a big smile. "It was done just as you planned. I had a great time with your niece. You told me she was a virgin, but I hadn't believed it!"

"What happened to your hand?" questioned Calvin.

"A small accident. Lost the end of my finger, but the girl was worth it." Eager to get it over with, Edgardo asked for the rest of his money.

Also, eager to get it over with, Calvin turned to reach for his hidden Colt. When he turned back, both fired. The heavy shot pushed Edgardo back. When Calvin realized he was shot, he leaned forward to see blood coming from his left shirt pocket. This enabled Edgardo just enough distance to reach Calvin's jugular vein with the knife in his left hand. As he slashed, both knew they were dead.

CHAPTER 25: THE TELEGRAPH AT SAN ANGELO

Brandon Cole felt comfortable that with his three cousins, Tommy Cole, Finley Cole, and Cliff Cole, he could find and kill Quick Tender. His thoughts kept going back to Texas Ranger Luke Shaw. What if he did show back up? He would not risk not accounting for him. He would go through San Saba and find the Pearl twins and hire them as his personal bodyguards. He had known of them to risk their own lives for those who hired them. They would be hired to keep Luke Shaw off his back until he could kill Quick Tender.

The Pearl twins were gun-slicks and operated on both sides of the law. If you had the money, they would work for you. They worked as a team and would not work individually. They were each six feet two inches tall with blond hair and blue eyes. They did not hide that they were killers but flaunted and were proud of it. Their clothes, saddles, and mounts were the best money could buy. Their presence often settled disputes without firing a shot.

After the Pearl brothers were hired, Brandon heard of the Indian uprising. This was another problem that had to be solved by Brandon. There was a significant Lipan Apache presence around San Saba. For years, the Catholic missionaries gradually converted the

Lipan Apache into Christianity. The Lipan Apache were worst enemies of the Comanche. Anytime they met, there was a battle.

Brandon Cole originally set out to get the Lipan Apache to accompany him to fight the Comanche while he sought Quick Tender. The Apache agreed until they found out that Cole was planning to kill Quick Tender, the man that had killed sixteen Comanche.

The only alternative for Brandon was misfit bandoleros that could be found in cantinas and around every village and trading post in Texas. They would do anything for money, ammunition, and tequila. Ten were picked up in San Saba, and twelve more were added on the way to San Angelo.

There was a chill in the air as the first cold front of the year slammed into the area around three o'clock in the morning. Quick had left his bedroll and coat inside. Not wanting to disturb her, he toughed it out. When Kathy Gale opened the door in response to his knock, Quick was standing with a load of firewood in both arms. Quick built a fire in the fireplace, and Kathy Gale fixed breakfast.

As a rider rode up, Quick was relieved that it was Sheriff Sterling. Over a cup of coffee, the sheriff told of Consuela Toro finding Edgardo Toro dead in her house and that it was apparent that Calvin had shot him in the heart with his Colt. It was also evident that Edgardo had shot Calvin in his heart with a Dillinger and slashed his throat. Both had bled out instantly.

Relief and sorrow flooded over Kathy Gale. Quick informed Sheriff Sterling that he had caught Edgardo Toro prowling around outside last night and of cutting off his finger when he reached for his knife. Quick had expressed his feelings that Calvin had sent Mr. Toro to kill him and Kathy Gale.

"You're probably right," said the sheriff.

"Sheriff, I will pay for Uncle Calvin's funeral, but I will not show up for the burial," said Kathy Gale.

"I understand, Kathy Gale," said the sheriff. "What are your plans, Mr. Riemens?"

"I'm going to hang around here until the rangers give an all-clear on the Indians. I realized how foolish I had been rushing off with Indians on the warpath."

"I'm certainly glad you were foolish, Mr. Riemens," Kathy Gale said with a smile on her face.

"Your plight was more incentive for me than catching up with Quick Tender," said Quick as Ryan. "Now that you are safe, I'm not near as excited about catching up with that guy. I don't think any of my competitors know him better than I, and I will be the one to catch up with him."

"That might be some hard-earned money," said the sheriff.

"I'm not doing it for the money," said Quick. "Any news from the rangers?"

"Only by word of mouth from people still just now coming in," explained Sheriff Sterling. "The Comanche have cut telegraph lines from Goldthwaite to Abilene and here. We haven't had service for the past three weeks. Don't know when the lines will be back up. The rumors are that the rangers are wiping out small raiding and hunting parties as they try to get back to the main tribe heading due west. It may take two or three weeks before the rangers give the all-clear."

Parting gestures with the sheriff were being made as Rocky Lane rode up. "Hi, Miss Kathy Gale."

"Oh! Rocky, I'm so glad to see you safe," exclaimed Kathy Gale. "How are Oliver, Earl, and Guy?"

"They're all safe," replied Rocky. "The house, barn, and the three-line shacks are safe. The bad news, Miss Kathy Gale, is that about half the herd was run off by the main Indian party, and there was nothing we could do to prevent it. We did good just to save our scalps."

Kathy Gale was visibly shaken, "Oh my!"

Quick introduced himself as Ryan Riemens, a friend of Kathy Gale.

"I know this is a shock, but on the bright side, everyone is safe, and the buildings are okay," calmed Quick. "Let's go in and have some breakfast, and you can make a plan to restock your ranch, Kathy Gale."

After breakfast, the discussion started, and Quick stayed out of the conversation until asked for his advice.

"Kathy Gale, you told me you had the best foreman and hands of anyone," stated Quick. "You have buildings, land, and water. Rocky, to your knowledge, have most of the Indians moved off most of the ranch?"

"We rode all over the ranch two days ago and did not see a single Indian," said Rocky.

"Kathy Gale, why don't you send Rocky back to the ranch, do a round-up, and get an actual count of the loss."

Before Kathy Gale could answer, Rocky spoke, "That's exactly what I think we should do."

"That's a good idea, Rocky," said Kathy Gale. "Pick up any supplies you might need and tell no one of our feared loss of cattle. Tell them only that all buildings and men are safe."

"It will take a couple of weeks. Is that Okay, Miss Kathy Gale?" asked Rocky.

"Yes, of course," replied Kathy Gale.

She then continued, "Oh, Ryan! This ruins everything. I won't have enough money to pay the hands for long unless I sell some of the cattle, which will make the situation even worse. How can I ever replace the lost cattle?"

"You are going to have a husband that has enough money to pay the hands, and as soon as I clear my name, I will have enough to triple the herd," said Quick with a smile.

"No one has that much money, Ryan," fretted Kathy Gale.

Before Quick could reassure Kathy Gale, they both went to the front door to see who was riding up in such a hurry.

Sheriff Sterling jumped off his horse with a big grin on his face and a long telegram in his hand, "Got some bad news for you, Mr. Riemens. Quick Tender has been totally exonerated of murdering the Cole brothers and breaking out of jail. Guess you did a lot of riding and hunting for nothing."

Kathy Gale and Quick looked at each other in surprise as the sheriff continued, "The bounty has been lifted off your head, uh—I mean Quick Tender's head, and all charges dropped. Brandon Cole has been kicked out of office by the Texas Rangers." The sheriff continued, "You will— uh, Quick Tender will now be honored as a hero for singlehandedly running the Comanche out of this part of the country. I received this telegraph just a bit ago and wanted to give you a heads-up. I will be distributing this news all over town and the county as soon as we get the all-clear from the Texas Rangers."

"Sheriff, this is great news!" exclaimed Quick. "Now all I, er, Quick must do is lie low until this news gets out to everyone. May I have that copy of that telegraph, Sheriff?" Quick asked.

"Sure! I have the printer printing off copies as we speak. If you run into Quick, let him know," the sheriff said with a wink and a grin on his face.

"He won't be around until all the bounty hunters get the word," reassured Quick.

"Don't blame him," replied the sheriff.

"Sheriff Sterling, thanks for having faith in me," said Quick.

"You bet I did, Quick," replied the sheriff with a handshake and a smile.

Quick and Kathy Gale rushed in the house, latched the door, and pulled in the string. They whooped and hollered, laughed and cried, kissed, and hugged.

Kathy Gale asked, "Quick, can we get married now?"

"Yes, but we need to go to Denver to get married," responded Quick.

"Why?" protested Kathy Gale.

"Brandon Cole may no longer be sheriff, but he is still vindictive toward Quick Tender," he responded. "I want to get Jo Ling and the crew here to cushion me from Brandon Cole, which will take a little time. Also, I want to distance Quick Tender from any talk or gossip about Salado or the Indians. I do not want credit for any of that. While we are getting Jo Ling here with the crew, I will make plans to rescue the ranch."

"Quick, I understand. I would love to rescue the ranch, but instead of putting money into the ranch, could we buy a small business in town that would give us a steady income?" she asked.

"Sure, we could, Kathy Gale, but I have bigger plans," replied Quick.

"Quick, I don't want us to be in debt," she responded.

"We won't be, trust me. How many cows will the ranch hold?" questioned Quick.

"Three thousand," Kathy Gale replied.

"I'm going to the telegraph office to try to get in touch with Jo Ling and take care of some other business. I will be back shortly. Would you like to go?" he asked.

"I'm in such a mess, it may take me a week to look decent enough to be seen in public, and it is so crowded there," she replied. "I would just be in the way. You go and be careful."

Quick gathered the Wells Fargo information to access his account and headed out. He transferred $45,000 to the Fort Worth Stockyard in exchange for 1,500 white-faced cows and twenty-five white-faced Bulls. He also moved $30,000 into Kathy Gale Chambers' Western Union account. He sent a message to several terminals, searching for Jo Ling. Quick was back by eleven. Kathy Gale trusted Quick but could not help but worry about their finances.

"Kathy Gale, it is a little early for lunch, but we need to go by Western Union first and your bank before lunch, and I don't want an excuse about how bad you look," Quick said the next morning.

"I thought you went there earlier this morning?" Kathy Gail questioned.

"I did, but you have a wire there," he explained.

"Wire for me?" she questioned.

"Wait and see," Quick teased with a smile.

Upon arrival, Kathy Gale was presented with a Wells Fargo check for $30,000. She was accustomed to picking up $1,000 checks for cattle sales, but $30,000?

"Quick, what in the world?" Kathy Gale asked with amazement.

Quick put a finger to his lips, grabbed her arm, and walked out.

"So you will quit worrying about money. Think of it as your wedding present from me. We also have fifteen hundred white-faced cows and twenty-five white-faced bulls being delivered to the ranch in two weeks," explained Quick. "I'm sure Jo Ling will be here by then. I've left him telegrams everywhere he might be. Let's go home and plan a trip to the ranch tomorrow and let Rocky know of the shipment."

When they arrived back at the townhouse, Kathy Gale went into the house, and Quick took the horses to the barn to water and feed them.

Echo was acting up. Quick turned just in time to see Kathy Gale being carried in front of a big man he recognized as a Cole. Another was following, five paces behind. Quick caught a shadow of one, at the corner, racing to the back of the barn. The one holding Kathy Gale had his Winchester in one hand. Quick climbed a rope to the loft with only three pulls. As the man raced into the barn, he let go of Kathy Gale to enable his effort to raise his Winchester and shoot whoever was flying toward him on a rope.

The bowie knife went in four inches below his navel and was withdrawn when it reached the solar plexus. It was reinserted at the bottom of the left rib cage and carved up and around the rib cage, severing the top of the stomach and finally exited at the bottom of his right rib cage.

The man dropped the Winchester so he could use both hands to hold his guts and stomach in his body, to no avail.

The man following behind got tangled up in the gut pile, then lost his footing and most of his head as Quick slashed out, severing his throat and most of his neck.

Quick turned to confront the third intruder and was shaken by the explosion behind his head. Kathy Gale had picked up the Winchester that had been dropped and shot past Quick's head, killing the third intruder.

Quick checked outside for others and found none. He went back in to comfort Kathy Gale. She needed no comforting. "They needed killing," she told Quick. Quick checked their pockets and found their names, Tommy Cole, Finley Cole, and Cliff Cole.

"Quick, they were waiting in the house when I went in. They grabbed me and covered my mouth so I couldn't alert you," she explained.

"We need to get out and into town," stated Quick. "Let's not be caught here until we know how many family members Brandon Cole has with him. If I can find him in a crowd, I will call him out." Quick continued, "If I call him out and kill him, and he has no more family with him, then it's over. I know I can beat him. Let me get my saddlebags, coat, and bedroll, and let's go." Quick put the coat on immediately.

As they were riding into town, Quick convinced Kathy Gale she needed to hide out until this was over. She wanted desperately to help but knew she couldn't. He told her of his room at the hotel and saw that she was safely inside.

Quick searched every street in town and then was convinced Brandon had to be across the River. As he crossed the wooden bridge, Quick saw Brandon Cole leading at least twenty men. Of particular interest were the two men closest to him. They were look-alikes. Both wore two long-barrel Colt .45s.

Without a doubt, Quick pegged the gunmen as the Pearl brothers, Brandon Cole's personal bodyguards. One was riding on each side of him. The rest looked like Mexican bandoleros, and all were wearing bandoliers of bullets across their chests. They all were on the left side of the street, heading toward him.

After seeing the bodyguards, Quick discarded his plan of having a showdown. He knew of a perfect place to have his battle with Brandon Cole. He would lead them into his trap.

Quick moved to the far right and made it to the first alley. There he had Echo rear up and cause a commotion in the street. Quick looked straight into Brandon Cole's eyes, making sure he recognized him, then raced down the alley and went north out of town. He slowed because Brandon had to get his small army across the street and on to the right trail. In ten minutes, he saw the dust trail of Brandon's forces more organized. Quick decided to leave a good trail and would go on to the location he had picked for the battle.

Quick arrived just at dark and circled and left tracks going in all directions. He staked Echo about a mile past the plateau and walked back with his saddlebags, canteen, and Henry rolled inside his bedroll. He cleared his trail as he went. He climbed up the plateau until he reached the protruding rock overhead and the crevice between the two rocks at the bottom. He was going to do his killing down below. This was just an observation point. His plan was to kill them all tonight. He snuggled in and went to sleep.

The small army woke him when they arrived about two hours after dark. They had a clear trail thus far. Now the trail was so mixed up, it would take daylight to untangle it. They stopped and made camp. Several small fires and one big one were started. It was evident that the camp was laid out for maximum defense. It was circular in nature with the highest concentration of cadre close to Brandon Cole.

Around the small, outlying fires, the men were seen heating their food to eat. The big fire hosted conversations and coffee drinking. He had located Brandon Cole the minute he rode into the camp, with the Pearl brothers at his side. One of the brothers prepared food for the other brother and Cole. Soon after eating, Brandon was led away from the large fire by one of his bodyguards. With his scope, Quick had enough light from the large fire to see several deep trenches that led to the arroyo. One of the trenches was cleared of brush and rocks, and saddles were placed so that Brandon

Cole could lie in between them. The saddles had been placed at the lowest part of the trench and close to the arroyo.

Brandon and one of his bodyguards lay down in the trench to sleep while the other stood guard close to the large fire but was always looking away from the fire. As the flame died down and the temperature plunged, the guard moved in closer and added more wood.

The attention of the gunman standing guard had waned as the temperature dropped and the fire got dimmer. Quick would wait until most were asleep but knew that some around the large fire would be assigned to guard duty throughout the night along with one of Brandon's bodyguards. The small fires went out, leaving only glimmering coals. The large fire was still hosting the occasional coffee drinker and the one gunman that was on duty at that time.

It was time to get started. Quick checked his weapons and eased back down the plateau. He left his saddlebags, bedroll, and Henry and would keep an occasional eye on them from down below. He had only taken an old sock that was full of previously wet shells from the saddlebag and put it in his coat pocket.

He had observed the formation and location of everyone from above. Their lines of defense were circular around the big fire. There were only five on the outer circle. He memorized all the positions and set out to eliminate the five on the outer circle and would work his way to the big fire, killing them all as he went. Sounds carried from the fire, and the sounds of the night grew louder. Quick would start with the man closest to him.

Inching along on his stomach and removing anything in front of him, Quick felt he was making good time in the pitch-dark night with only the flickering shadows from the fire. He came to his first target. He reached around the small tree, grabbing the nose and mouth of his victim and reached around with his right hand, ready to cut his throat. He stopped and froze in position. He realized the man's head had already been half severed. A thousand thoughts went through his brain. Had the man had a quarrel with one of his compadres? That's the only conclusion he could come up with. Quick moved on to his next target. He was within four feet of his next target when he froze. He did not hear or see anything, but just knew that someone was looking at him. After about two minutes, he heard his name being whispered.

"Yes," whispered Quick.

It was Boris. They moved together back from the outer circle at least two hundred yards. Still whispering, they talked. He told Quick that he, Fazio, and Paul followed him from Goldthwaite to San Angelo. When there, they saw the posting that he had been cleared of all charges in the Cut and Shoot incident. Jo Ling, Ross, and a Texas Ranger by the name of Luke Shaw sent a wire in hopes that we would pick it up in San Angelo. The wire said they were hot on the trail of Brandon Cole. They knew Cole was out to kill Quick and asked if we could help until they could get here. "We think Jo ling, Ross, and the Texas Ranger are close. The Texas Ranger wants to kill Brandon Cole because he told him he would personally kill him if he or one of his bounty hunters messed with you."

"Boris, I can't let anyone fight my battle for me. I'm mad, and I'm ready, and I plan to kill them all tonight," demanded Quick.

"Quick, listen!" exclaimed Boris, "Brandon will be just as dead if you let Luke Shaw do it."

"I'll just wait and see how it plays out," mumbled Quick.

"I couldn't find you, but I did see Brandon Cole leaving San Angelo. I told Fazio and Paul I was going to tag along," explained Boris. "I knew they were after you, and that you were near. I thought I would just go ahead and take out their outer circle, which I now have done. Now, we should wait for the others."

Quick spoke up, "I've one other thing to do. I won't be firing my gun, but there will be a lot of firing going on. You might cover me from the north if need be. I'll meet you at the southeast corner of the plateau afterward."

Quick moved back to the body he had found. He removed the large sombrero and the poncho from the dead Mexican. He turned the poncho inside out to cover the bloodstains, then slipped it on. He then put the sombrero on and pulled it low over his eyes. He picked up the dead Mexican's rifle and started toward the fire, stooping to as short as he thought the Mexican might be. He greeted the gunman and the one Mexican at the campfire in Spanish, bent over, and dropped the sock in the hot coals. He picked up the coffeepot and raked the coals over the sock and poured the coffee in a cup. He then set the pot on top of the coals that covered the sock, tasted the coffee, and exclaimed the coffee was bitter. Quick threw it out and stormed off into the darkness. When he got back to the body, he removed the sombrero and poncho, ducked down, and moved north to the rendezvous point.

Quick led Boris up the plateau to his lookout. Both could see through the gap in the large stones. When the first bullet in the sock fired, it sent the coffeepot sailing in the air, spilling hot coffee on the gunman. The gunman standing guard thought he had been fired on and moved away from the fire and fired at the first movement he saw.

A loud scream came from his target that got off a shot before dying. The Mexicans standing next to the fire also thought they had been fired on from the same direction and started shooting at anything that moved in that area, which brought more shots from that direction.

The bodyguard lying in the trench with Brandon raised and shot at them. More explosions coming from the sock sent shrapnel in all directions, some mortally wounding those nearby. The gunman that had been on guard fired to the right and then to the left of the returned gunfire while moving away from his own muzzle blast. This brought more targets toward him as the Mexicans fired back. Everyone started shooting at other men shooting back at them.

Quick had his eye on the bodyguard that had been on duty and saw a volley of shots hit him. The bodyguard emptied his two guns, shooting at anything that moved before he fell after having his legs cut from under him by shrapnel from the fire. He was now taking fire from several directions. The gunman was on his side, reloading his Colts and still firing at every shot fired at him. He had been shot to ribbons by the Mexicans and struck numerous times by pieces of shrapnel. He was now firing from instinct. His last two shots were made with direct hits into two approaching Mexicans, one in the chest and one in the stomach. With guns empty, the gunman was still pulling the triggers when he rolled over dead.

The other gunman had risen from Brandon Cole's side and had not had to deal with the shrapnel from the fire as had his brother and the Mexicans close by.

There was a loud scream from one Mexican, "Mueren los gringos," as he rushed toward the gringo. He had only run four yards before he was shot and fell dead. The gunman moved after every shot and reloaded at will. He was still firing and moving ten minutes after the first shell exploded in the fire. The guard was first hit by rifle fire that came from the direction of the outer circle of the defense. It hit him in the shoulder that knocked him to the ground. He decided to get back to the trench and get Brandon Cole's help in stopping the bleeding. He had stuffed the bullet hole in front with his bandana but could not reach the back. When he had crawled close to the trench Brandon was in, Brandon fired and killed the guard. He had kept the muzzle of his gun out of view from the

Mexicans. He killed the guard for fear that the guard's nearness to him would draw the Mexicans' fire to him.

There were moans of pain and continuous firing from the entire area. Mexicans shooting at Mexicans. Prayers could be heard, and after some shots, screams from the recipients were bloodcurdling. Late explosions were still coming from the fire. Brandon Cole remained in his hole and pulled mesquite as thick as he could over himself.

Screams of the wounded still filled the air. One raced to the fire and screamed out to stop firing. He was shot when he let out his second scream. It would be several hours before it would be light enough to determine the outcome below.

Quick had previously planned to leave the lookout before daylight, not wanting to be trapped on this side of the plateau. After discussing this with Boris, who was positive that Jo Ling, Ross, Paul, Fazio, and Texas Ranger Luke Shaw were already in position waiting for daylight, the decision was made to sit tight. Moans from the wounded were heard throughout the night.

Quick was looking through his telescope even before it was light enough to see. Gradually, he could pick out some of those that were killed and wounded. One was seated rocking back and forth as if in a daze. He was sitting next to one that was obviously gutshot, moaning, and writhing on the ground. He counted eight dead, not counting the five Boris had killed on the outside prematurely. He counted four others wounded. Finally, he picked out Brandon Cole. He was still in the trench leading to the arroyo with mesquite foliage pulled over him. One of the Pearl brothers lay dead ten yards out facing him.

"Hello, camp. This is Texas Ranger, Luke Shaw. Throwdown your guns."

The sitting wounded Mexican that he had seen earlier pulled out his gun and shot his gut-shot friend in the head then blew his own brains out.

Quick got sight of Jo Ling. Quick put the Henry to his shoulder, stood up, and caught Jo Ling's attention. He pointed out the position of Brandon Cole. Jo Ling signaled Quick to sit tight.

Shortly, all of Brandon's gang were accounted for, dead or wounded. Luke Shaw walked toward Brandon Cole's hiding place, and Brandon threw out his gun and stood. He started telling Luke how glad he was to see him.

"I don't want to hear it, Cole. Pick up your gun. You are going to need it," stated Luke.

"Why? I'm giving up," Cole whimpered.

"I said, pick it up. I told you if you messed with Quick Tender, an innocent man, I would hunt you down and kill you," said Luke. "Well, I've hunted you down, and I'm going to kill you. I'm going to give you a chance to defend yourself, you lying scumbag."

Brandon dove for his gun and was raising it before Luke stepped to one side where he pulled his gun and fired the shot before Brandon could. As big as Brandon Cole was, the slug he took in the right shoulder knocked him back into the trench. He struggled to get his gun up as Luke Shaw walked closer, still telling him how sorry he was, then shot him in the other shoulder. Luke hesitated, then shot him in the stomach and stated, "This will be the last cross you will ever see, Brandon," then shot him between the eyes to finish the cross.

"Luke, meet Quick Tender," said Ross.

"Son, I'm sorry for all you've had to go through because of this crooked lawman. This ordeal is finally over for you. I don't want to do all the paperwork on this and want you and your family here to forget this final episode. You'll go back to San Angelo, and I'll clean this all up by myself. You will never hear anything about it because it never happened, you hear?"

"But, Mr. Shaw, I have three bodies of the Cole brothers in a barn in San Angelo."

Luke interrupted him. "No. You don't. It's been taken care of.

That never happened.

CHAPTER 26: THE RECEPTION IN DENVER

Quick and the crew rode back to San Angelo together. He filled them in on Kathy Gale and the wedding in Denver. He asked them to attend and be in the wedding party. They all agreed.

Quick also shared with them the information he had received concerning the railroad. He asked Jo Ling to arrange the trip to Denver and prepare to leave as soon as possible.

After reaching San Angelo, Quick rushed to see Kathy Gale.

"I knew you would be back," said Kathy Gale with tears rolling down her face.

"It's over, Kathy Gale, totally over." Another round of hugging, kissing, laughing, and tears of joy took place. That night, they fell asleep in each other's arms.

The next morning, there was so much to tell Kathy Gale, he felt he had to rush to get it all in.

"We will catch a train in Lorain," explained Quick

"Quick, the train doesn't stop in Lorain," corrected Kathy Gale.

"Trust me, the train will stop in Lorain," Quick said with a smile.

"Okay, I will always trust you, Quick," she replied.

"Jo Ling will have seamstresses and haberdashers on board with all the supplies and accessories needed to make and complement clothes for the wedding party. By the time we get to Denver, we all will have new wardrobes." Quick continued, "We will go by the ranch on the way to Lorain and tell Rocky to prepare for the cattle shipment and tell him of our plans. We will leave in the morning."

It was only a one-day ride to the ranch using the road on the east side of the Concho. By leaving at daylight, they arrived just at dark. Rocky had just gotten there and was surprised but glad to see them. Rocky was told about the cattle and the marriage. Quick assured him that the operation of the ranch was entirely in his hands. Then he gave Rocky a list of things he wanted him to do.

One was not to worry about cost. Quick told Rocky that Kathy Gale had told him her hands were the best around and that he wanted them paid as such. Quick also suggested to Rocky that he should hire several more hands to better look after the more expensive cattle. Quick wanted him to give any Indian that was hungry as many cows as needed, and he would replace them. Any cowboy that was hungry and asked for beef was to have it. If they stole it, hang them. All this was music to Rocky's ears. Quick told him that he and Kathy Gale would be all over the country, but Jo Ling would always be available to get in touch immediately if needed.

Upon arriving in Lorain, Quick and Kathy Gale were escorted to a private railcar. Jo Ling and the crew would have a private car located in front of theirs. Jo Ling had arranged to have a special car for Echo and the other horses and another for the three seamstresses and two haberdashers to work in. When the conductor informed them of this, Kathy Gale started to protest but decided to wait until the conductor left.

"Quick, how in the world can we afford all this?" questioned Kathy Gale

"Kathy Gale, the railroad is paying for most of this," explained Quick.

"But why, Quick?" she questioned.

"Let me explain later. I have a wedding to plan," Quick replied as he began to write out several wires to be sent to Denver.

Jo Ling had arranged the appointments for measurements by the seamstresses, and upon arriving in Denver, each had a completely new wardrobe.

Kathy Gale had her wedding dress, and several ball gowns, shoes, hats, and gloves included and a complete traveling wardrobe. The guys had their tuxedos, hats, and shoes.

The concierge for the hotel picked the entourage up at the train station with carriages and escorted them to their hotel suites.

"It has been a whirlwind, sir," said the concierge. "The governor has requested invitations for him and his entourage of twenty."

"Of course, and send him my special greetings," replied Quick.

That night, Quick and Kathy Gale had dinner served in the suite. Quick was ready to tell her of his wealth. He had not told her before because he had not truly known of its vastness.

It seems the railroad had been trying to get in touch with him for over three months. Quick was told that he was now the largest stockholder of the railroad. This occurred when the two railroad companies that his grandfather had bought stock in merged. His grandfather had voted on the merger, not knowing it would make him the largest stockholder in the new company, owning more than 66 percent of the stock.

Captain Drake had bought the stock before the railroads were built and continued buying stock for the rest of his life. His grandfather had never taken any dividends and had plowed the money back into the company by buying more stock. With 66 percent ownership, Quick now could call all the shots for the company. It was a vast and profitable railroad. There was also a large amount of gold on deposit with Wells Fargo with easy access. Kathy Gale did not grasp everything, but she could live with it.

The wedding went off without a hitch, except that it was very crowded. The party afterward was the largest ever held in Denver. The women stood in line to meet Kathy Gale. Quick was near, being greeted by the governor, railroad executives, bankers, and everyone that was somebody. Quick also sought out the servants and custodians. He introduced himself and thanked them for their service.

Kathy Gale and Quick slipped to their suite around midnight. Jo Ling was to meet them there at seven the next morning. Breakfast was served in the room. After breakfast, Quick dismissed the servers. Quick, Kathy Gale and Jo Ling sat alone at the table.

"Jo Ling, first, I want to keep our family together. Kathy Gale had no family, and now she will be part of ours. Do what it takes. We were all lost when we broke up after Captain Drake's death."

"It will be easy," Jo Ling replied.

"Here is what we want to be done. Assign the crew as you wish," Quick said as he handed Jo Ling the list.

- Buy this hotel and increase the size of the ballroom. If they won't sell, build one nicer and bigger.

- Jo Ling will be appointed the chief operating officer of the railroad. The railroad is using the Colorado National Bank. Buy them out. If they don't want to sell, build our own bank and transfer all the railroad business to it. Jo

214

Ling is to protect the minority stockholders. They can vote to be included in these purchases or be excluded. If excluded, use my money.

- Buy the Rancher's Preferred Bank of San Angelo.
- Buy a mountain nearby that has good access, a creek or river, and large building sites.
- Find the best doctor in the country and move him to Denver. Kathy Gale and I are going to have a house full of kids.
- Find the best house builder that knows how to build a house in the mountains. I will have Kathy Gale lay out what she wants, and she shall have what she wants.
- Hire Luke Shaw. I want him as our family security guard. I like his attitude.

"Jo Ling, get Luke here as soon as possible. Kathy Gale and I are leaving for California, and we will be back here to have our first baby."

Kathy Gale knew she had caught her bounty hunter!

ABOUT THE AUTHOR

Bert Lindsey was born, reared, and resides in Texas. He graduated from Kilgore College and the University of Houston. He has been an entrepreneur in Oil, Lumber, and Real Estate. He says he has lived his life thus far with many principles set forth in western novels. His two favorites are *Your Word Is Everything* and *Don't Be Bullied by Anyone*. He wants his readers to see, feel, and be emotionally involved in the surprises, tensions, romance, and happiness that *Quick Tender* offers.